THE FIDDLER IS A GOOD WOMAN

To my favourite ukelele player David Francis

THE FIDDLER IS A GOOD WOMAN

keep writing please

Love

a novel

Hastings 2018

GEOFF BERNER

DUNDURN
TORONTO

Image creditst: © Carolyn Mark
Printer: Webcom

Library and Archives Canada Cataloguing in Publication

Berner, Geoff, 1971-, author
The fiddler is a good woman / Geoff Berner.

Issued in print and electronic formats.
ISBN 978-1-4597-3708-2 (softcover).--ISBN 978-1-4597-3709-9 (PDF).--
ISBN 978-1-4597-3710-5 (EPUB)

I. Title.

PS8603.E7353F53 2017 C813›.6 C2017-901848-5
C2017-901849-3

1 2 3 4 5 21 20 19 18 17

Conseil des Arts du Canada | Canada Council for the Arts | Canada | ONTARIO ARTS COUNCIL CONSEIL DES ARTS DE L'ONTARIO an Ontario government agency un organisme du gouvernement de l'Ontario

We acknowledge the support of the **Canada Council for the Arts**, which last year invested $153 million to bring the arts to Canadians throughout the country, and the **Ontario Arts Council** for our publishing program. We also acknowledge the financial support of the **Government of Ontario**, through the **Ontario Book Publishing Tax Credit** and the **Ontario Media Development Corporation**, and the **Government of Canada**.

Nous remercions le **Conseil des arts du Canada** de son soutien. L'an dernier, le Conseil a investi 153 millions de dollars pour mettre de l'art dans la vie des Canadiennes et des Canadiens de tout le pays.

Care has been taken to trace the ownership of copyright material used in this book. The author and the publisher welcome any information enabling them to rectify any references or credits in subsequent editions.

— *J. Kirk Howard, President*

The publisher is not responsible for websites or their content unless they are owned by the publisher.

Printed and bound in Canada.

VISIT US AT

dundurn.com | @dundurnpress | dundurnpress | dundurnpress

Dundurn
3 Church Street, Suite 500
Toronto, Ontario, Canada
M5E 1M2

All music is what
awakes within us when we
are reminded by the instruments;
It is not the violins or the clarinets —
It is not the beating of the drums —
Nor the score of the baritone singing
his sweet romanza; nor that of the men's chorus,
Nor that of the women's chorus —
It is nearer and farther than they.*

Lovingly,
Eunice Waymon
Age 12
(later named Nina Simone)

* The poem is written by Walt Whitman; Simone included it on the back of her album *Here Comes the Sun.*

CAST OF NARRATORS

(IN ORDER OF APPEARANCE)

Geoff Berner: Author. Singer/songwriter/accordion player who occasionally played with DD.

Campbell Ouiniette: Former music manager of various folk, punk, country and "world" music artists. Narrator of the book *Festival Man.*

Amy Williams: Singer/songwriter/guitar player. Founding member of DD's old band the Supersonic Grifters.

Jasmine McKittrik: Professional life coach.

Mykola Loychuck: Singer/songwriter/kobza player who toured with DD.

Pete Podey: Drummer, played with DD.

Name Withheld: Belfast poet.

Miruna Molnar: Nutritionist, moved to Galiano Island to be with DD.

Carla Patterson: Strip bar owner, childhood friend of DD.

Giulietta "G" Caetano: Singer/songwriter/guitar/banjo player. Replaced Amy Williams in the Supersonic Grifters. Later recruited into the band the Low Johannas.

Tom Abbott: Singer/songwriter/guitar/mandolin player, open mic host, formerly in the Supersonic Grifters.

Lila Austin: Singer, songwriter. Former lead singer of the Low Johannas.

Kris Hauser: Former guitar player in the Low Johannas.

Melanie Schiff: Former recycling worker. Former career criminal.

IMPORTANT INTRODUCTORY NOTE

Dear Reader,

This book is a document of my failure. I will explain:

The song "You Are Home to Me," by the Low Johannahs, was a hit in eleven countries. The official video has been viewed on YouTube over eight million times. Numerous acts, large and small, have recorded their own version, notably the pop star Spe$ha.

This has led to a great deal of interest in the song's author and composer, a woman known as DD.

What is DD's "real" name? I suppose "real" journalists would delve into that, but I'm not a journalist, or even a reporter, and I make a policy of calling people what they would have me call them and leaving it at that.

Fan interest in DD has been fed by the circumstance that nobody seems to know where she is.

A missing persons case was filed in Winnipeg in July 2012, the day after she walked away from her band's tour bus at two in the afternoon, saying she was going to get a pack of cigarettes. The Winnipeg Police were unable to find any leads. Members of her band voiced frustration at what they saw as a lackadaisical tenor to the official search efforts, and speculated publicly that the officers' zeal might have been dampened by the fact that she is a woman, a musician, and of Indigenous heritage. Those kinds of people disappear all the time, after all.

In a twist of corporate kismet, my publisher, Dundurn Press, picked up the rights to the publishing and recording revenues from "You Are Home to Me" when they were able to buy most of the assets of Moevment Music at a fire-sale price, after that once-legendary recording, publishing, and management company went bankrupt. I understand that Dundurn mostly bought it for the sheet-music rights.

I had been struggling to write a follow-up to my first book, *Festival Man*. Dundurn asked me to write a "quickie bio-book" about DD, since she appears in *Festival Man*, and I have, in fact, played with her on many occasions.

They also suggested that I make some inquiries to see if I couldn't actually locate DD, since it would certainly be a coup to score the first interview with her in years. Also, Kirk Howard of Dundurn is that rare animal in business, an ethically punctilious man, and it troubled him to be holding almost half a million dollars' revenue from "You Are Home to Me" in a trust account.

So I set out to do all that, to write the bio-book, to find the fiddler. And this book is the record of my giving up. I failed to write the book, and I failed to find DD. Well, after I failed to find her, I sort of found her, briefly, in a manner of speaking, but not really, and in a way that did not diminish my failure, in my opinion.

I take full responsibility for my failure, which consists of a combination of a lack of daily discipline, as well as what I hypothesize to be a lack of insight into truths that might have been revealed to a more observant and deductive mind.

Over the course of a few years, in my travels as a touring accordion player/singer-songwriter on the independent folk- and world-music circuit in North America and Europe, I interviewed many people connected with DD, and collected a great deal of material. I was not able to make a coherent, digestible biography out of it.

Instead, what I offer here is a boiled-down version of that maddening mess of material, organized by me and my trusted editor, Shannon Whibbs. We did our best to throw out the boring bits, and keep the stuff that might be of interest to fans, or to anyone with more adept powers of detection, who might glean a clue as to DD's whereabouts.

I miss her very much. That is all.

Yours,
Geoff Berner

CAMPBELL OUINIETTE

BEGINNING OF REJECTED FORTY-PAGE ARTICLE, SUBMITTED TO *BC MUSICIAN MAGAZINE*, 2015 (POSTMARKED MACEDONIA)

OF COURSE I'M NOT DEAD. Reports of my demise have been horseshit. As was that whole book, *Festival Man*, that Berner wrote, claiming that he was "deciphering" my handwriting from my report on the Calgary Folk Festival. Pretty fucking creative deciphering. There's *tons* of shit in there that I never wrote in a million years. Now I hear he's out there trying to write something about that little gap-toothed fiddler, the one they call "DD." Well, I wish her luck, because he sure did a hatchet job on me.

Well I don't know where to begin. For example, he's got me calling *him* a "lying Jew bastard," as if I would be stupid enough, in this day and age, knowing what I know about how this world actually runs, to write something like that for public consumption. Although in essence, when it comes to the reality of what he did to my reputation with that book, what can you say? If the little black dress shoe fits …

Among the many lies the book tells that I want to go on record about are:

- I never said that the Artistic Director of the Calgary Folk Festival, Leslie Stark, was "semi-autistic" in her insensitivity. She is a rugged individualist, much like Yours Truly. She pulls no punches. As per same. That's not autism, that's Albertanism.

- I did *not* know for sure that Athena Amarok was not going to fulfill the contracts we had made with the festivals in the summer of '03. When I spent the advance for Calgary and the other advances (on perfectly legitimate expenses, I might add), it was in full expectation that she would be holding up her end of the bargain.
- There's no way I would have run from a conflict with Big Dave McLean in 2003. Because by 2003, Big Dave had quit drinking. Sure, when he was in full liquor mode, in the old days, I once saw him jump on the roof of a Winnipeg cop cruiser outside the Royal Albert Hotel and rip the sirens off it with his bare hands. But by 2001 he was sober. A non-violent, Gandhian pussycat. So that proves I would *not* have been intimidated by him.

Also I did *not* spit on Stan Rogers's widow at the Stan Rogers Festival. Although I do despise the song "Amazing Grace," which she had chosen as the Grand Finale number for the festival, where everybody gets onstage and sings Kumbaya-style together. I truly despise "Amazing Grace." People say Christianity is a Slave Religion, but I'd say it's more like an *Overseer's* Religion, and that nasty little ditty is like a manual for the whole Christian Empire — do a ton of horrible shit, grab the goodies, keep 'em, ask God for Forgiveness, and then, you know, just call it even and no hard feelings all around, right? So in a way, it's a *perfect* song to sing as the Grand Finale on the mainstage at the end of the Stan Rogers Festival, now that I think of it. But I never spat on Stan Rogers's widow. He *was* a phony-baloney manufacturer of fake "Canadian" culture that got overplayed on the national radio station for Imperial purposes. But I never spat on his widow.

Plus there's a whole shit-ton of stuff Berner got wrong about my exploits during the Siege of Sarajevo, and he probably put some people in grave danger because of that. There's just a whole shit-ton of stuff that you can check against the *historical record,* and the chain of events he describes just don't add up. I'm not going to go into it. It's just horseshit. That's all. After a book like that, it's pretty clear nobody in their right mind ought to trust Geoff Berner, ever again.

Who would have thunk that a book like that would be such a success? Bestseller lists in Europe, sale of film rights, etc. I'm pretty much certain that Berner's holding out on me for some of the royalties, although I can't prove it. The man has a lawyer's mind. And I *don't* mean that as a compliment. He's got a weird way about dough. It was always difficult getting him to pony up front for my grant writing and other services. Yet he never seemed to get evicted or have to pawn his instruments, like a lot of my clients over the years. Frankly, I suspect there's some sort of family money there. I can smell it. I see him and his soft hands, and his suspicious tendency to never look you in the eye, and I think, *There's a man who's never had to really work for a living.* Now he's getting all these accolades, he's getting a big head, but let's face it, as a prose writer, he's not much more than a two-bit Canuck Kinky Friedman.

Anyway, as you can see, I have not expired, and I never contemplated throwing myself in the river or whatever. Berner just left the story "open-ended" for the sake of pretentious drama, I'm sure. He's threatening to become one of those "I don't provide answers, I just ask questions" *Artiste* types that I despise. If he hadn't written one or two decent songs, I would never have dealt with him at all.

I just needed to clear out of Dodge for a little bit, to let things cool down for a while. I called Dugg Simpson, artistic director of the Vancouver Folk Festival before the ungrateful board of directors shitcanned him (don't get me started about boards of directors). I called Dugg before I left town. I asked him how bad the fallout had been from everything that happened that summer, and he said — I'll never forget this — "You could not see the sky for smoke from bridges burning." So, yeah, I figured it was time to give Canada a break from Cam Ouiniette. So people could remember how much they missed me.

In case you people don't already know, Berner is out there looking for DD. He's written to me via snail mail here. I can't say exactly where I am, for several reasons, but I'll go so far as to reveal that I'm somewhere in the Balkan Peninsula. Berner found me somehow and sent one of his grotesquely twee little missives, full of five-dollar words and hyperbolized mock-politeness, like a Chinese gangster in a 1920s private-eye story.

He wants my help looking for DD, because, in his words, he reckons that I have "the deepest working experience of anyone I know at effectively going to ground." How do you like that? Cheeky sonofabitch.

Well if he wants my help, he can fucking whistle for it, as far as I'm concerned.

It's funny, when DD was just another pointy-toothed vagabond rounder, for years she was well and truly lost, but nobody was trying to find her. Like most poor people in this world. Then she writes a hit song by accident, and suddenly she's a mysterious recluse.

Well fuck that. If she wants to be left alone, I say leave her the fuck alone. And that's all I've got to say about that.

But I will say, if you're looking for a fiddler, you have to think like a fiddler. Berner knows what that means. Or he ought to.

Erratic. Psychologically wounded. Let's just say it straight: crazy. They all are, fiddlers. Instruments select for certain personality types. That's a scientific fact. Violins are tiny wooden boxes stretched by cat guts till they almost break. Then you drag the hair from a horse's tail back and forth over it, and you're supposed to make music with that. Beautiful music is *expected*, and there's no hiding in the background, like with a bass, which determines the groove of a band, but which no one actively listens to besides bass players and strippers. Here's a riddle: How many bass players were at the party? Answer: Who cares? The fiddle is the opposite. It keens away in the high mid-frequencies, like a mother's voice, so everybody who ever had a mother is biologically attuned to listening for it.

And of course there's no markings on a violin to tell you where the hell the note is supposed to be. No frets. You're just supposed to *feel* where your fingers should go. With your *ears*, mind you. Fuck. If you're not insane when you take up an instrument like that, you will be soon enough, and history proves me right on that score. Think of Nero, just as a for-instance.

Like the sound of the violin itself, fiddlers' mental health statuses skidder all over the place on their way up and down and around the intended note. And have you seen how much fucking sugar a fiddler puts in her coffee? Jebus.

So like I say, if you're looking for a fiddler, think like a fiddler. Which of course Berner can't do because *he's* another breed of fish entirely. Singer-songwriter, which is hardly even a musician at all, mostly. You think Berner could get hired as a sideman accordionist? No way. Not good enough. Singer-songwriters have a whole other type of being. Absent-minded, self-absorbed, *sensitive*, but not to the right things that might help them get along in this world. Most of them are relatively genial people, unless they're in the presence of somebody who might help their careers, in which case they all turn into terminally grumpy dickheads, determined to show their fierce independent-mindedness, but just coming off as surprisingly ignorant assholes.

I say *most*, because of course there are exceptions, like Cole Dixon, still my favourite country guy, who's a very astute businessman, but Berner's not one of those. He's a garden-variety, daydreaming, self-sabotaging singer-songwriter. Good luck catching a fiddler with a screwy mind like that. For all we know, she's been leaving him clues left, right, and centre and he's just been too obtuse to notice. That's a very real possibility.

Of course, DD is not your ordinary fiddler. That's true.

Anyway, getting to the main subject, the state of folk music festivals in Canada today …

AMY WILLIAMS

HER KITCHEN, FERNWOOD NEIGHBOURHOOD, VICTORIA, 2014

WE SPENT OUR TWENTIES RUINING each other's relationships. One of us would get some kind of long-term thing going and then we'd wind up looking in each others' eyes too long, then we'd just have a little smooch, and sure enough we'd be fucking. Cheating. Repeatedly. Until we got caught. Inevitably. We did that about seven or eight times before we finally tried shacking up together, which, of course, did not work.

I'm not saying she was always the one to blame about the ruining thing. One time somewhere in the middle of those years of ruining, I went over to her house she was renting with this chick in Fernwood in Victoria, I don't remember who she was with at the time, but I was just so goddamn horny for her. This had been going on for what felt like weeks, where — I just could not stop thinking about her, and I just went over there in these boots I knew she'd like, and a really short pleated skirt and her girl was not there, and basically I got down on all fours and just begged, "please, *please* just fuck me," over and over till she just couldn't stand it anymore. So, that one was kinda my fault, I guess. [Laughs.]

Of course I'll always love her, even though she put me through so many flavours of hell over the years. And I wish her the best, wherever she is. And I really have no clue. You know that, right, Berner?

If you came to me hoping I'd be able to help find her, you're barking up the complete wrong tree. Have you checked every single island in the Strait of Juan de Fuca? Because she's an island girl. I can't decide if it's because she needs to be near the ocean, in order to feel calmed by the great vastness of it, the way it puts a person's petty little problems in perspective, or if she just feels most at home when she can see trouble coming from any direction, so she can make a break for it. She always keeps access to some kind of little dinghy or something. An island is like a fortress, but it's also something you can escape from quick in a boat, and leave your pursuer behind, standing on the dock, shaking their fist. I know about that because she turned me into that person for a while. And fuck her for that. Fuck her.

I was already attracted to her way before I heard her play. She's actually a very pretty girl, if she lets you look at her the right way. She must be the grand champion of making missing teeth seem sexy. She just has this special way about her. Any way I can think of to describe it just sounds silly or clichéd. What's a clever way to say she has a twinkle in her eye, when she actually has an honest-to-God twinkle in her eye? What's a clever way to say she seemed to be holding a magic secret that she was thinking about maybe sharing with you, when that's just exactly how she is? I don't know. I'm a songwriter. I don't pretend to be a poet.

So, I was already into her before I heard her play. But then, when I heard her play, that was it. Boom. Oh my God. I'd never heard anyone play that way before. It made me realize exactly what it was that I was trying to do when I sang and played guitar, but I hadn't known it was okay to play that way. I was so afraid of doing it wrong, of messing up. But DD's playing was never afraid of that.

If you want to understand DD's way of playing, I'll try to tell you the best I can, but I have to tell you a story, so you have to be patient. All right?

Ever watch one of those shows that's all over the TV, like *American Idol*, or *The Voice*, or *The X Factor*? The talent-contest shows where they "discover" new "stars." Well, a couple years ago I was over at my auntie's, and one of those was on, and you know how TV can just be on, but you're not really watching it, but somehow, without realizing, you really *are* watching it? Intently. And these poor little fuckers, most of them *kids*, but some of them people like me in their thirties now, but who never gave up on *the dream*, the dream of "making it," they're singing these fucking stupid songs that people have heard a million times, like a Billy Joel song or whatever. They are just so fucking, fucking eager to please. They know they're being judged. And they know that other people will decide if they're a "real singer" or not. They want to impress. They want to impress the judges, they want to impress their parents in the audience, they want to impress the audience. It's so fucking sad watching these shows. Some of these singers can really hit those crazy high notes, and swoop around, and falsetto like a beached dolphin and everything. I mean, they can really *sing*. Technically. And some of them know it. But they don't sing in a free way, in a true way. Because the way they sing, you can feel that they want to know if *you* think they can sing, too.

Then the show was over, and they hadn't picked a winner yet, but Auntie and me pretty much knew who was the best singer and all, and *so what?* was what we were both thinking, without saying anything.

Auntie turned off the TV. She said, "Come on, let's listen to this old record I've got. It's got your grandmother's favourite song on it," and we went into her living room.

As she went through her collection, looking for it, she said, "You know, your grandmother hated doctors, and she didn't go to the hospital till the neighbour came by and found her lying on the couch, moaning, with a bulge in her tummy like she was pregnant and half to term. They rushed her to emergency and she never left the hospital again.

"When we used to go to the hospital to visit her, I would bring my little portable record player and she would always say 'Play it. Play my favourite song,' and I would play a 45 I had of Frank Sinatra singing 'My Way' and she would close her eyes and listen, and when it came to the part where he would say, 'let the record show, I took the blows', your grandmother would always do the same thing, where she would scrunch her eyes up tight when he sang, 'let the record show, I took the blows,' as if she was taking the blows right there. And we knew she was thinking of your mother and our big brother, who she wasn't able to keep from being taken away, and how she finally managed to get them out of there, unlike many who didn't survive. You could see it all on your grandmother's face as he sang 'let the record show' and then she would take the blows, and then Old Blue Eyes would take a breath and just let it rip with '… and did it … my way —' and her face would just relax. She would mouth those words and she would escape, escape from the pain for that little moment where she and Frankie sang 'My Way' together."

My auntie reached into the record collection of beat-up LP jackets. They all had those yellowish circles that get worn into the old white covers from the inside out, you know, from the disks pressing on them over the decades. She pulled out a record with no title on it, just an image, a yellow and orange painting of a sun.

"And then exactly a year after we'd buried your grandmother," Auntie said, "I saw this record in the Kelly's, and the cover kind of caught my eye. I looked on the back of it, and there was a picture of a homely black girl on it, not a pretty lady like Diana Ross or Lena Horne (don't get me wrong, I love those ladies). And the last track of the second side was 'My Way.' So I went to a listening booth, and I put on the last track of this album and just listened. It's my favourite song, my favourite record of all time, and I'm going to play it for you now, Amy."

Then Auntie played the record.

I don't know if you've ever heard Nina Simone's version of "My Way," but it kicks the living shit out of Sinatra's version. I'm not against Sinatra's music, although I hear he was an asshole in life (but who wasn't?). Sinatra's version is like a boxer who just came out of the ring. He took some shots, he got knocked down, sure. And now he's gonna retire, but he basically won. He persevered and he won. He's the Champ.

Nina Simone's version is not like that. Without telling me anything about it, I knew what Auntie was saying when she looked hard at me, as we listened to the record. Auntie was telling me that when she played Sinatra's version of "My Way" for my grandmother when she was being eaten alive by the cancer, my grandmother, in her mind, in her soul, was actually singing Nina Simone's version, even though it hadn't been recorded yet. And I understood that my auntie was telling me this without her having to do anything at all but look at me as the record played. Do you understand what I mean?

You go out and buy that Nina Simone record with "My Way" on it, and you listen to that after watching a whole hour of one of those fucking shows like *American Idol* or *The Voice* or whatever. And you listen to Nina Simone. And you will hear, without any doubt, how Nina Simone does not give a single, tiny, living fuck what you or anybody else thinks about how she is singing that song. She is *in* the song, she *is* the fucking song. She heard Sinatra sing it, and she took it, and said, "That's *mine.* I will express the things that *must be said* through this song. Because they must be said. And it will not be 'perfect.' And you will hear what I have been through. And you will feel it."

That's how DD plays the violin. Like that.

JASMINE MCKITTRIK

DHARMA LODGE, GALIANO ISLAND, B.C., 2015

OH, WELL, YOU KNOW, DD has a lot of issues. I should know. I just want to say for the record I was her first real love. I was the first real marriage-like partnership she had, and there's still no one who has been with her longer than me. I guess the work I had to do when it came to DD, the lesson that was there for me in *my* journey, was that we are responsible for our *own* journeys, but not for everyone else's.

I gave a lot of love to DD. I put a lot of work into us. DD, frankly, did not. But I don't think the work I did was a waste, because, ultimately, I know we are going to be together again. There have just been too many signs of that, over the years. I don't feel comfortable talking about them. They were extremely intimate signs. But I feel like when she's learned what she needs to learn, that's when we'll be able to pick up again where we left off, but further down a path of wisdom.

What does she need to learn? She needs to learn patience. To not just run around looking for something that's not to be found, like how she's obviously run away from her problems *again* recently. Obviously she needs to learn to just be still, and mindful, and feel where she is at the moment. And she needs to work on being less selfish, and she needs to confront some of her — excuse me — shit. Life shit that she's afraid of confronting. She's still totally in denial about a lot of the things that happened in her childhood. Look, I'm telling you that I have done a lot of work with people who suffered abuse, and I always offered to work with her, and she was very resistant to just letting me get right in there and help her.

Our connection happened before I ever heard her play. It was not about "oh, I'm going to be with this rock-star violinist" or anything, for me. Our connection was deeper. In a way, her music was like a disability for her. Because it was a distraction from the real work she needed to be doing. She could go off into her music, and I would be like, "Hello? You really need to put down that thing and *look* at me, and *deal* with some of the shit that's holding you back here," and she would just clam up, or take off on the road, for weeks and weeks, leaving me to just — what? Sit around on this island and *wait* for her? And then she would finally come home and be fucking sick, from all the *toxins* she would put in her *body* while she was out there drinking red wine and smoking *cigarettes* with Rosalyn Knight and eating literal shit at *Burger King* with Brody. Then she would want to be *babied,* and she'd want to be *mothered,* and then she'd sleep for like, three days, I'm telling you, like, really, three *days* of being just a rumpled roll of bedclothes where you were thinking, *I need to poke this person and just say* are you even alive?

And then there was all the cheating. Why not call it what it is? What *she* is. She *is* a *cheater*. That's just who she *is.* That's another way her music really held her back, in a lot of ways. Because every time she came off the stage, like *everywhere,* there was always some wide-eyed little (I'm sorry, but it's true) slut running up to her and practically *begging* for her to fuck her. Everywhere. Even times when I would be there, and she would dedicate a song to me from the stage, they would still come. I don't have a lot of great things to say about Rosalyn Knight, but she got it right when she called DD the "gateway lesbian." I couldn't tell you the number of times girls ran up to her and told her, "Oh my God! I only just realized I might be bisexual just now! When I heard you play the violin!" No, honestly. I'm telling you. They would *say* that when I was right beside her. With my arm around her.

So, you see it would be so very easy for me to say, hey, I don't bloody care where she is. I hope she rots in hell. She is a liar. You reap what you sow. But in fact, because of that, frankly, instead I actually feel extremely sorry for her. I believe in love above all things, and I know that our destinies are intertwined in a very, very deep way. We are soulmates. And at some point in time, when she's ready, when her journey has taken her where she needs to go, I still believe that we will one day be together. That is all I have to say.

MYKOLA LOYCHUCK

GREEN ROOM AREA, RUDOLSTADT-FESTIVAL, RUDOLSTADT, GERMANY, 2015

WHAT DO I REMEMBER ABOUT DD? Uhhh, so much … [long pause]. It's very difficult to start because … I don't know how to organize it in my head … and I have several theories about DD, and I'm worried. I'm concerned that some of them may contradict each other.

Well … [long pause]. One is that sometimes, I genuinely believed that God had sent her to this planet to teach me patience. She had this way of showing up for the plane, or the train, or the show itself at the very last second, after I'd checked in with her exactly a hundred thousand times to make sure she got there an hour ahead of time, just to allow for a margin of error. But she didn't believe in reserving anything for a margin of error. I think my heart is at least … eleven years older from the wear and tear of wondering if she was actually going to show up at all. Although, looking back, she always did. So, does that mean that she was always, in her way, trying to get me to stop worrying? Or did she enjoy watching me sweat?

What else?

I read a science fiction book once. I don't remember what it was called … Wait. It's possible that this is a dream that I had and not a book that I read.

In the book, or in the dream, there were people whose minds had fused with cats. There was a woman, a regular human woman.

She was leaving the outer-space town or something, going away. She asked her lover, who was a person who had fused with a cat in his mind, she asked him if he would miss her after she left, and the cat person said something like, "Meow ... how can I think about you if you're not there? Meow."

All right, well, perhaps that's an overstatement of sorts, but she ... she's very in the moment. This is what makes her such an excellent side player. Not even a side player — side player isn't a fair term for her.

She forces you, the singing songwriter, to come into the moment with her, to reside in the song and not think about anything else. God what a sweet mercy and a triumph that can be when I can do it. When I can connect to my own humanity through a song, and then I shock myself that I'm actually connecting with other human beings. It's the greatest thing.

Of course all the self-help new-age books all demand that you live in the moment. But what if you actually do live in the moment, which I have done sometimes with DD over the years? You wind up not remembering things that you told people you were going to do, including some promises you made, and you wind up not remembering things you promised you *weren't* going to do, and you forget about planning any plan for the future, because you're so living in the moment.

Although everyone says we are supposed to do that, it is actually something that annoys people a lot, to say the least, when you do it. I have experienced this from several different angles ... [long pause]. Yes, I have.

She claimed to be a direct descendant of Chief Sitting Bull. He's the one who beat Custer at the battle of the Little Bighorn. Oh, you knew that. Of course. I didn't mean to insult you ...

She told me she almost earned a degree in classical music from the conservatory, but they told her she would have to wear a dress to the final recital, so she just didn't go.

She claimed to be born with a crescent wrench in her back pocket. She said it many times. She loved anything with wheels and she claimed to be able to drive and fix anything with wheels, from a backhoe to a grader to a locomotive. Could be. I once watched her hot-wire a cherry-picker truck in Whitehorse at four in the morning and drive it down the street to a mini-mall where we got in it and she got us up to the roof and we drank vodka out of Big Gulp cups and looked at the Northern Lights.

I was fretting aloud about how we were going to get arrested and I was trying to figure out a plausible story to tell to the cops to explain about why we were on the roof of the 7-Eleven with a weird stolen truck, and DD said, "Just shut up and look at the lights, boss." I said okay … and took a deep breath, and just looked at them and almost enjoyed them like a person is supposed to. We didn't get arrested. The cops never came.

She claimed … she claimed to have hacked into the website that ran the Royal Bank of Canada bank machines in her hometown, and that she caused the one near her school to spit out a twenty-dollar bill every weekday at noon for all of grade nine.

She claimed that when she was a child, her father would sit by the window during dinner, with a .22 rifle. She claimed that he would shoot rats in the woodpile as they ate.

She claimed to have been raised by Jehovah's Witnesses with no notion of a birthday party or Christmas presents.

She claimed that her parents didn't force her to play the violin, like most people who ever played the violin. Instead she said it was the other way around — she said that at the age of four she had seen Itzhak Perlman playing a violin on TV and demanded to have one. She said that for three years every time she passed the music store she would scream and cry and carry on, until her mother finally relented and got her one and then only begrudgingly paid for lessons from the only teacher in town.

Other times she claimed that her first instrument was the tuba, at her mother's insistence, and that her parents would send her up the ladder with the tuba to the attic to scare away the bats.

She was always DD, but she was always whatever version of DD she needed to be, or whatever version of DD she felt was required. So sometimes, if we were playing at a hippy festival, she would go full hippy and let some girl talk about whether Sagittarius was compatible with Aries as the girl braided her hair. Then the next night we might play at a Legion in the neighbouring town and she would go full redneck, talking with some manly man in a lumberjacket about favourite chainsaw brands, telling him about the time she was eight years old and had to drive her dad to emergency when his Husqvarna jumped and bit his shoulder.

Sometimes she would be in an intellectual mode, where she would reveal that she'd read *A Brief History of Time* in an afternoon. But then if we were out partying with her partying buddies, and you asked her, hey, what did she think of that book she'd been reading in the van, she might just say, "What do I think? I think I'll have another Kokanee."

She always lived on some island or other, and in my experience there were always at least two women she had … she had, she was having — one for home and one on the road. Sometimes the one from the road would replace the one at home, thinking that now she was going to be the only one, but then not that long after that, there might be another one on the road. And of course this sometimes led to … problems. One show we did, a girl I'd never seen before paid full cover just to come into the community center gymnasium and stand perfectly still through the whole set, staring at DD with her middle finger high in the air. But then she probably went home with someone else again that night. She could pick up like I've never seen.

One time we were in Nuremberg and I was wearing a hat that I didn't like. It had started to bother me, like a canker sore, you know, in the lower back left of your mouth. It was making me kind of tense and hard to be around. I only forgot about it when I was playing the shows, because I never wear a hat when I'm playing, unless I'm sick. I was looking for a new hat. I had a black hat and a brown thrift-store suit that fit me. I hadn't known that you weren't supposed to wear a black hat and a brown suit until some girl told me that, in a way that informed me that I had descended in her estimation because of the colour of my hat. I was feeling very sensitive on that tour, so my hat was really bothering me at this point. I couldn't shake it. We went into the bar next to the little theatre where we had played. I saw a hat that looked like mine, but it was brown like my suit and I thought maybe it might fit me. It was hanging on a hook behind the bar, quite high.

A pretty girl was bartending. She had mostly short hair but what do you call those? Tufts. Long side tufts. And a little tail at the back. She had more than one piercing on her face. I had been thinking about going over there and trying to start a conversation with her, but I was only on my second beer. I didn't know yet if I would be able to work up the courage and the disregard for the fact that generally girls don't like to get hit on while they're working. Sometimes I disregard it and then, of course, I feel disgusted with myself the next day, or even as soon as later that night.

I said, "gee, that looks like a better hat than what I've got," and DD said, "gimme that" and walked over to the bartender girl with my hat.

I couldn't hear what they said but the girl took the hat down, and tried on my hat. It fit her quite well. DD said something to her and the girl said something to DD. DD brought the brown hat to me. I asked her what the girl had said about the hat, and DD told me she'd said that she got off work in an hour and asked if DD had a place to stay.

In previous conversations, we had both agreed that generally when people ask touring musicians if they have a place to stay, they are at least thinking about fucking them, even if they haven't discovered in their own minds yet that that is what they are thinking. Not that someone will necessarily fuck every musician they ask "So, where do they have you staying?" but they are often rolling the thought around in their mind. So I said, "Oh. I see."

I tried on the hat but it didn't fit very well.

The next day we met up with DD at the train station. I asked her if she'd had a good time when she went home with the pretty bartender, and DD said yes but that it had been a little weird because she had a boyfriend.

"She told you she had a boyfriend?"

"No, I met him," she said.

"He was there when you got there? How did he feel about you being there?"

"He was pretty sad because when we arrived, we all chatted for a while and had a beer and then she took him into the other room and broke up with him."

"She took you home and broke up with her boyfriend?"

"When we were in bed later she said that she'd been meaning to do it for a while, and I was just the … what's the word for something that makes something change, like with rust?"

"The catalyst," I said.

"Right. She said I was the catalyst. Her English was very good. And she speaks French, too. We mostly spoke French together."

I told her I hated her. That made her laugh.

The rest of the tour, we had a running gag where we would call her "the Catalyst," as in "the Catalyst really needs to dig out her passport because we're approaching the Swiss border," or she might rub her belly and say, "the Catalyst is ready for a big plate of kartoffels." Or someone would ask, "has anyone seen the Catalyst?" and the answer would be, "the Catalyst is in the men's can because some big Austrian woman in the ladies' room mistook her for a boy and screamed at her," or something.

PETE PODEY

HIS HOME STUDIO, BASEMENT SUITE, GRAVELY STREET, OFF COMMERCIAL DRIVE, VANCOUVER, 2014

I'M RECORDING NOW. Check. Check one two. Levels look good. Okay, this is Peter Podey, July 27, 2014. I'm recording this because Geoff has asked me to try to come up with some thoughts about DD. Ah, for the record I don't know where she might be. I wish I did.

What can I say about DD? Okay, well, I love her. Not in a sexy kind of way, although of course she is sexy, that's just not the nature of our thing. I love her. Like a sister? Yeah. Like a sister, or maybe like the way guys in a platoon in a war love each other, because they've been through so much together, they've saved each others' lives, they've seen each other at their worst and their best, and they have a deep respect. I don't know if this is helpful. Okay, I'm just gonna roll on into this microphone, and you can, you know, do whatever you want with it.

Yeah. A deep respect. And that really begins because of the way we play music together, which is hard to explain. We really communicate. Okay, well, that doesn't even come close to what I'm trying to describe, which is a really amazing thing, you know? "We really communicate" sounds weak compared to the feeling. DD understands what I do, and I understand what she does. A lot of people *kind* of get how special DD is. But it says something special about her, that she also gets what I do, because that's not as common, for whatever reason. Actually no, okay, because there's a good reason for that.

I'm not sure where to start about it, but I guess I'll start with how I met her, and that leads me to Geoff's book, I guess.

So ... I really enjoyed Geoff's book, or I guess Cam's book, or whichever. Ha ha. It was a lot of fun, and I understand that when someone is writing a whole book, things get edited out and everything, for space.

And I don't want to make a big deal out of this or anything, because it's not a big deal, and I guess it's a matter of ego, or something, and that's not really how I like to live my life. The thing is, in that book, there're a lot of things that happen in it where, you know, I was actually there.

I don't mean there in Calgary, or there at the festival. I mean in the room. Participating in the discussion. And in the book it's like I wasn't there. Actually like there was either no drummer at all, or else he has Jenny drumming, when, if you get right down to it, she was playing bass. Jenny *is* a great drummer, but, you know.

Like I say, I don't mean to say that somebody has done some kind of terrible thing to me by leaving me out of the history of what was happening, but I just need to say for the purposes of telling you about DD that, for the record, I was there.

I was the drummer for the Athena Amarok project that summer. Cam specifically asked me to do it because he'd admired my old band and he liked what I was doing there. I guess he liked the portability of my set-up, too, which took a lot of work, a lot of trial and error, to fit right into a suitcase, unlike a lot of drummers that have to have this huge kit and everything. I mean you couldn't have put Neil Peart into a situation like that and fit his stuff into a rental minivan.

For instance, right there at the start of the story I was in the minivan with Mykola and Cam and Jenny when we were zooming over the Rocky Mountains toward the Calgary Folk Festival. I was holding the map in the passenger seat. I was looking over the distances between cities on the back of the map, comparing the driving times between Vancouver and Calgary and Vancouver and Edmonton, comparing them to my own personal experience driving to Alberta from the coast. I say that just because I remember exactly what I was doing when Jenny shouted at Mykola to slow down and Mykola jammed on the brakes. My travelling water bottle can be a bit too big for the cupholder in some of those minivans — if you drive smoothly it's not a problem, but, to be fair, it was a bit precarious. So the contents of the water bottle spilled all over the map, and all over the front seat, and Cam didn't mention that part in his story, or else Geoff maybe couldn't decipher that part of his handwriting, I guess.

There's a fair number of parts of the book where I was there like that, and I'm just not mentioned anywhere, so yeah.

This is something that happens to me a lot, I have to say. I know it's partly my fault. Probably my fault. Maybe because I'm the second youngest in a family of six kids, and I've always wanted to be a drummer, or I've always *been* a kid who drums, like since I can remember. I am a drummer. Of course I'm a human first, but I experience the world as a drummer. Probably only other drummers will understand what I'm talking about.

I was always practising, even when I didn't have a stick in my hand. Everywhere I was, I was always tapping out paradiddles and little patterns with my fingers, and it just bugged the heck out of my mom and my older siblings and my dad, too. When I was quite young, when they would notice me tapping, they'd get irritated, and you know how kids can be. They'd slam down on my hands to stop me tapping. You know, like, "STOP that tapping!" and it would really kind of hurt. I still remember it now. So, I kind of learned how to practise without anybody noticing.

That's how I developed what DD calls "Pete's incredible superpower of invisibility," which is really something where I can virtually disappear from peoples' consciousness and still be right there, doing my thing. I mean, I don't even think about it now. I almost have to work to turn it *off*, so that I can actually have people pay attention to my opinion or let me contribute to a decision that's being made. It's a power that's really benefited me over the years, but maybe also led to me not always getting noticed or credited by people for the things I've done.

Or servers at restaurants will forget to take my order when I'm out with a group at dinner, and I'll have to say "excuse me" a few times or maybe even get up and tap them on the shoulder to get their attention.

Or I'll be up onstage and I'll notice there's actually no drums whatsoever in the monitor, and I'll have to get the singer to shout into the mic that the drummer needs his wedge turned up with more of him in it. And the tech will say "drummer?" and kind of look at me like he just saw me teleport onto the stage out of nowhere, even though I introduced myself to him earlier in the day.

I'm not saying this for my own horn-blowing here (although okay, maybe partly I am … I mean, I don't claim I don't have an ego. I mean, that would be silly because of course I have an ego; everybody does). But I'm just doing this because Geoff specifically asked me to talk about DD. Here's why:

I actually met DD before anybody else did, when she and her band — what were they called? The Speedy Zippers? The Supersonic Grifters. Right. Anyway, I met her first when they were busking outside the Calgary Folk Festival gates, because I was kind of tapping along on the fence and DD noticed me.

She noticed me. Right away. She looked at me just grooving, tapping the fence, but doing it in my own way, which is that the first thing in my mind is how to serve the song. How to make a rhythmic contribution that helps the *song*. It sounds obvious, but actually most drummers — I'm sorry, maybe not most drummers … well, actually, yeah, sorry, most drummers — are kind of thinking more about their own playing, and whether or not they're being cool, or "check this fill out" and that's fundamentally not what I do, as a drummer. I serve the song. I love, *love* great songs. Sometimes I serve the song so much that people don't remember there were drums, and in a way, that's a compliment. But true musicians hear the drums and get what I'm up to. And when I was only just tapping on the fence, DD locked on my eyes. She locked right in with me and shared a part of herself with me. I know that sounds kind of hippy. Sometimes Mykola mocks me for being a little bit hippy but, to be fair to him, he wouldn't mock me about that, because he knows about this stuff, too. That's why we play together. And I looked back at her, and she gave this little nod. And I knew what that nod meant without either of us saying anything, and what it meant was, "I see you, you're a real musician. We're making something together now."

I know that sounds silly, but actually it's completely true, and I stand by it. My invisibility power doesn't work on DD. She sees me as who I am, which is a damn good, song-sensitive drummer, an artist. Not to toot my own horn too much, and I realize that the more I say that, the more I'm undermining what I'm saying, which is super frustrating for me.

[Pause.]

I'm just saying DD saw me. Right away. I was never invisible to her. I don't know if that makes sense but anyway that's what I wanted to say. Okay. I know I was supposed to try to think of clues about where she might have gone, and I don't think I've really done that. I'm going to take a break, and I'll try to say more later.

JASMINE MCKITTRIK

DHARMA LODGE, GALIANO ISLAND, B.C., 2015

AS I SAID, IT TOOK ME A WHILE to truly figure her out, but I now clearly see DD's music thing for what it was: a way for her to disconnect from people who were close to her, a way to step away from the real work of communicating with people, heart to heart. It was her armour, and, of course, an excuse to not really grow up. That's sad. But at one point, I totally fell for the idea that music was this magical thing that made her magic and all that false wisdom.

I mean, after she played, people would look at her like she was some kind of priestess or something, like she had access to a special, special spiritual thing. And I'll admit that at that point in my own journey, I may have been jealous. I can admit that now.

Now, I mean, now at this point in my life, that all seems pretty amusing to me, since I'm now at this point in my life where, as a shaman myself, people come to me to help them through their journey, help them work on themselves, and I'm not ashamed or afraid to say that yes, they're willing to pay a significant amount of their wealth-seed to make those changes happen in their lives. I often have people asking to pay *more,* because, I'm telling you, they tell me themselves that the work we do here has been so invaluable in their lives. But I don't wish to get off track here. What I'm doing here is trying to tell you a story about how lost we both really were, in some ways, at that time in our lives. How this idea of musical ability as some kind of window on wisdom, well, frankly, it fooled both of us.

I had started to take up the violin, not because DD played the violin, but just because I loved it. I thought that maybe I might have a special connection with it because my great-uncle had played the violin at one time in a symphony in England. Whenever he came over to our house in Kitsilano I always tried to just hold it, but of course my mother was always afraid I would break it so I'd get my hands slapped each time I reached out for it. Please, don't get me started about the repression I had to deal with in that house. Later they did get me lessons but by then the repression of the earlier incidents had marked me, and there was so much else to deal with that I was never really able to apply myself. This is why later, when I was living with DD on the island, I thought I should maybe try again — to regain what I had lost.

I got a hold of a violin at a pawnshop in Victoria, without telling her, of course, and it came with a bow, and I was very keen on practising. The first time I pulled it out and started doing some scales, DD was out visiting someone or fucking someone or something, I don't know, but then she came back, she came into the house, which was more of a cabin, really, and the first thing she said was, "Hey, who's ass-fucking a Siamese cat with a hot poker in here?"

Which I should have expected, really. That kind of derision. It was typical of her when it came to music, which, of course, was *her* exclusive domain.

But I persevered. I kept up with my scales, despite the faces she made, despite the way she would run for the front door when I reached for the case. I also worked on an exercise from the Suzuki Method, a lullaby by Brahms, which gave me comfort sometimes. But it certainly gave no comfort to her. She would visibly wince every time I even mentioned the violin. She even stopped playing the violin herself in the house. And I missed that. I really did.

Then she went on tour with Mykola for a while, and I slowly lost interest in it. It was just too hard, knowing how she was judging me the whole time, making hurtful comments like, "God in Heaven, are you trying to kill me?" or "Hey, you know if you reach a little higher on the scale, you'll hit the Brown Note. That's the one that makes people shit their pants."

So I set it aside, sadly.

Then one summer we were at the Vancouver Folk Music Festival, and I had a chance to see this incredible man named Xavier Rudd. I'm telling you, talk about magic. This golden-haired Aussie played some kind of guitar that he would actually play on his lap, *and* he sang like an angel, *and* he played the didgeridoo. Simultaneously. Often, he would layer his sound using this amazing pedal at his feet. Honestly, I still to this day don't know how he did it. And he sang the most beautiful songs about the beauty of the Earth, and about the treasure of Australian aboriginal culture and wisdom. The crowd was understandably enraptured, and I was among them. This may sound unbelievable, but, honestly, those of us who were ready to feel his message? Were transported thousands of years, to the time of the Dreaming.

I dragged DD to hear another of his performances at the same festival, but she was too blocked to get him at all. "Isn't he *amazing*?" I asked her. But I sensed some jealousy coming off her. She just said, "Yeah, that's a neat trick he's pulling off there."

I pointed out to her the incredible way he had completely mastered the circular breathing technique that allows aboriginal holy men to play these hollowed gourd logs perpetually, without stopping to inhale. "Yeah, I bet he can use that for lots of things," was her only response. But I was literally enraptured. I felt a special connection to the didgeridoo in particular, partly because of my unusually spiritual nature and my understanding of aboriginal spirituality all over the world, having studied it intensively over the years.

But I should have expected that when I brought one home, her only comment would be, "Oh, my fucking God."

I was telling some friends at a gathering that I'd begun studying it, and she ducked into the room with a beer in her hand just to say, "I like to think of it as a didgeri-don't. Ha ha," then she let out one of her huge, disgusting Kokanee beer belches.

I was determined not to let her judgment get in the way of my personal development. So I practised and practised. It was genuinely, extremely rewarding on a lot of levels. But one thing preyed on me, and it was really a hard thing — I was unable to quite make the kind of sound I really wanted with it.

I would play and play, but the most I could get out of it was a kind of *woof* sound. Or sometimes I'd use my own technique and simply call down into it, calling down my deepest and most honest feelings into the ancient wood. But it never quite felt satisfying, and a lot of the time I wound up having to lie down for an hour after practising, because it makes you really light-headed.

I persevered, and she persevered in undermining me. "Don't tell me you're still blowing on that log," or "You know that women aren't allowed to play those things?" or "Why don't you come to bed. I'll give you something you can put your mouth on and blow." She could be so crude.

But the caustic remarks weren't what eventually stopped me. It was something she did, late in our relationship.

One day, I had been practising in the practice room in our little house. She had initially thought of it as *her* practice room, but now that I was playing, I was booking time to practice there, too. I had been there for about an hour. I was blowing as hard as I could, and still, not really approaching the sound I was trying for.

That's when she did it. She stormed in. I'm telling you, her face was like a contorted mask. "I can't stand it. Gimme that thing!" she shouted, and literally snatched my instrument, this sacred object, right out of my hand. I tried to take it back, but she shouted, "Back off! Right. Watch this, dammit!"

She put her mouth on it. She blew. She made a perfect sound. She modulated the sound. She turned it into that classic "ah-wa-wa-wa-oh" reverberation, making it rhythmic. It sounded exactly like Xavier Rudd. She did it for nearly two full minutes as I watched.

Then she dropped it. "There. See? Not so hard. Do it like that. Okay?" Then she stormed out.

I didn't speak to her for four days. She knew she had done wrong, and she tried to make amends, but I knew then that this phase of our lives together was over. I never played again.

NAME WITHHELD

BELFAST, 2013

WHAT I RECOGNIZED ABOUT HER right away was that she had been raped. In her life, she had been raped. I don't know if everybody who's been raped has this ability, but when I've talked it over with others who are living through the aftermath, the aftermath which is your whole life, it's been something we felt we could notice. Obviously I don't spot every single person and sometimes I'm wrong. So I never walk up and announce it to the person. I just wait and am not surprised if they tell me about it after a while.

You might doubt yourself when you think you see it, but deep down you know when you see somebody else who's living through it. Call it *rapedar*. Ha. I know I shouldn't laugh but you've caught me on a difficult day … should I go on? You seem a bit uncomfortable.

Right, so, my rapedar spotted her. 'Cause here's how it is, like, when someone is *doing* that to you. Your mind is shrieking, "no, no, no," and you're looking for some kind of escape, and you realize that there is no escape. You are in a nightmare. And the man who is raping you, or the men who are raping you, as in my case, are laughing at your pathetic search for an escape, because you are seen as an amusement toy, and you are thinking, "Why doesn't somebody help me? Why is there nobody here to help me?" But there *is* no one to help you. You have been selected to have this experience of complete and utter powerlessness, of men laughing in your face while you are powerless.

Perhaps if it happens when you're a small child, then it's a different matter. Perhaps then, the world of rape is the only world you've ever known. I don't say that I speak for anyone except myself, but I suppose I must have been raised with some expectation of safety, or perhaps not safety but autonomy, because afterward, well, I began to see the world very differently than before. You begin to see the *people* around you very differently.

Because you're looking around yourself, and you're thinking, That *person didn't help me.* That *person didn't help me.* In particular, you see people in authority, people like teachers and headmasters and headmistresses and police and priests and nuns and *parents* and you think to yourself, She *couldn't protect me.* He *couldn't (or wouldn't) protect me,* as you look at all these people who are in your world who are supposed to have your best interests in mind, to keep you safe, to do things *for your own good* and you think, *What an unbelievable load of shite that is.*

And you find yourself surprised, caught off guard, by how very, very angry you are indeed.

Because while the rape is happening, it's like the world has been turned on its head. You've entered a new world of betrayal where people are getting real enjoyment out of doing you harm. You think, *This can't be happening.* It's like the world has been turned upside down.

But then you look around you, and you start to see the world, and you begin to think, no, the world didn't just turn upside down. This *is* the world. The people who are supposedly there to protect you and others, they don't, in reality, do that. Many of them are *part* of it, part of the people who think it's funny when they can make others feel as if there's nothing they can do but have harm done to them.

And so when I say that I spotted DD, when I connected with

her that afternoon at the pub, that's what I mean, what I saw. I saw the anger. My sort of anger. Not boiling beneath the surface, but *right there* in plain view. If you have it yourself, you can see it in others — the way she held herself, the way she held something back behind her smiling eyes. It's the anger of knowing that the world is not simply imperfect, not simply needing a few nice alterations so it can be just grand, just peachy — the anger of knowing that the world is completely upside down.

AMY WILLIAMS

HER KITCHEN, FERNWOOD NEIGHBOURHOOD, VICTORIA, 2014

OUR BAND LOVED ROSALYN KNIGHT. We loooved her. Why did we love her? Oh, come on. You've toured with her. *You* know. All right, all right. Let me count the ways.

She was quick. She still is. Always ready with a snappy remark for any occasion. I remember sneaking backstage at Roots Fest mainly just to see her in action. We had just made it in back there. We saw some hippy volunteer come up to her and say, "Do you know there's no smoking here?" and, like a shot, Rosalyn replied, "No, but if you hum a few bars I can play along." Later, in the beer garden, some hipster CBC guy shouted, "Hey, Rosalyn, Minnie Pearl called, she wants her outfit back!" and she just shot back, "Hey, Grant, Don Rickles called, he wants his jokes back." The chick from the Cowboy Junkies had snubbed her, and *that* was a big mistake because Rosalyn was the MC. They were taking a long time to set up before their show. She leans into the mic and broadcasts, "Boy, for a band that made its best record fifteen years ago with a single microphone, they sure have a lot of gear to set up!" Saw her come off the stage when she opened for k.d. lang at the big theatre. "Thanks very much! It's been a pressure!" Somebody asked her what she had in her setlist one night before she went on at Tuesday's — "Gonna play a medley of my hit."

Yeah, we worshipped her. She was cool. She dressed in awesome thrift-store cowgirl clothes. She always had a smoke and a glass of red wine going. She was the only woman we knew who was making a living playing music. She was doing it. And we could *see* her. She was at the bar. She was at the Market on Yates buying spinach. She was riding her bike past the bakery. You know? And she wrote fucking amazing songs. "I'll Make You Pay For It," "Column A and Column B," "Duchess of Esquimalt." Holy shit. We would buy her albums and take them home and try to learn the songs. They seemed pretty simple and hummable, but when you took them apart, this shit was *complicated.* DD would have a little notebook and she'd just scratch out a mark every time we came to a new part of the song, and it'd be like, "Oh, shit, she didn't go back to the *A* section, and she cut the bar in half before that — how many sections has she done? Six? This is the *F section of this song*. Jesus, what a woman." That was how we felt about Rosalyn. She was our hero.

She didn't really know us. We were just little punk kids to her. One time after we'd learned a bunch of them, we got shit-faced for courage on Golden Wedding and showed up on her doorstep at 3:00 a.m., and played five of her songs in a row. By song three she came out in her pyjamas, glass of red wine in her hand, and just smoked and drank and listened. Brody, her guitar player, came out and she just said, "Look what the sexy children are doing on our porch!" When we were done she invited us in for snacks. She gave us wine and made bruschetta. We got so drunk she let us crash on the floor of her living room. As we lay down she said, "John Carroll spilled a bottle of Talisker Special Cask on that floor last night, so if you get thirsty there's probably seventy dollars worth of whiskey you could suck out of the carpet."

I told her that, to us, she was like a mix of Nelson Mandela, Beethoven, and Simone de Beauvoir or something. I said if there was ever anything we could do for her, we would crawl over broken glass for her, we'd do anything for her. Without skipping a beat, she exhaled her smoke and said, "Got a place I could park my van for three months?"

She needed somewhere to park her Plush Monster, an '82 Ford Econoline that used to be some kind of BC Hydro service vehicle and then got "customized" by some dude who clearly dressed it up to lure high-school girls. It was a beautifully creepy thing. She was going to Europe with Mykola I think, some trip out to Scandinavia or something. It was the kind of awesome glamorous thing that she did. Of course she could park her van with us! It was an honour.

So later when we realized that if we were gonna be real musicians, we had to go on the road, and we realized we were gonna need a vehicle, we just looked out the window at the driveway, and DD said, "Yep."

When Rosalyn got back, I approached her at the Hullabaloo Open Mic at Tuesday's about buying her van. "Are you sure?" she asked. I offered her five hundred bucks for it.

"Okay. Send the funny little fiddler kid with the missing teeth. Tell her to meet me on the bench at Beacon Hill Park at high noon on Sunday. Tell her to have the five hundred, in cash, in a paperback book. I'll have the van papers in a book. We'll do the switch there." Rosalyn always had to do stuff as if she was a spy. I'm not sure why. At the time she didn't even have a bank account, so The Man couldn't track her down. She was an outlaw.

DD and I went to Russell Books, the used bookstore there on Fort Street, and looked for the perfect book. We found a pulp soft-porn novel from the fifties called *The Timid Virgin*. That seemed appropriate, since we were tour virgins. As a band, we'd never played further away than Duncan.

When DD returned from her "clandestine" meeting, the book she had with the papers in it made us feel like the van was a Vehicle of Fate. It was a paperback from the same series as *The Timid Virgin*, called *The Happy Hooker*. In the book's margins, Rosalyn had handwritten a list of bars and house concerts that spanned the country, along with their contact numbers. How we vibrated over that. The whole exchange had been done in complete silence. They had both worn hats with brims that covered their faces. Looking back, I think Rosalyn was already recruiting DD, back then, for various purposes. She was laying tour eggs to catch a future road dog, for sure.

On our way to the ferry, we stopped at Chambers Towers to say goodbye and thanks. It was 1:00 p.m. Rosalyn came down, bleary-eyed, in her bathrobe. "Oh, you're going now? All right then, kids. Have a good tour! Drive fast, take chances! Safety third!"

JASMINE MCKITTRIK

DHARMA LODGE, GALIANO ISLAND, B.C., 2015

PEOPLE CAN BE NEGATIVE IF THEY WANT TO BE. If that's how they want to perceive reality. It's sad, but some people, so many people, still haven't figured out that we create our own realities with our minds. This has actually been proven by physicists at the big Halon Collider in Switzerland. You manifest things, and they happen. And if you manifest gossiping, and always criticizing, well, you know, you're going to have a negative life, very frankly. And you only have yourself to blame for that. You manifested it. I've made several trips to India, and in India, let me tell you, the amazing people I met, they understand this. People who manifest negativity there are called *Untouchables* for a reason. You know, there's a story about an old First Nations grandfather and his grandson, and I'm not going to tell the whole story but basically the grandfather says you have two wolves inside you, fighting each other in there, grandson, and one of them is the positive, "Yeah! Let's do this!" wolf, and the other is the negative wolf with negative attitudes, the envy wolf, the always-seeing-the-glass-half-empty wolf. And they're fighting. And the grandson says, "Which one is going to win, grandfather?" and the grandfather says, "The one you feed." Aha? See what I mean?

I don't have time for that kind of negativity. I don't feed that negative wolf. I think the reason that some people talk negatively about me can be summed up in one word — the green-eyed monster: *jealousy*. At this point, my life is pretty self-actualized. I travel, I lead seminars. I get a lot of time in nature, which really recharges me and connects me to the Earth. I don't mind if people call me a hippy. That's their damage. I get things done. I don't smoke the weed at all now, and even back then I certainly never smoked as much as DD used to, probably still does.

I was the one who found the houses we lived in. I was the one who made sure the rent and hydro bills got paid every month. I was the one who took her to the doctor's when she inevitably came home sick from tour. I was the one who held her tight through her freak-out nights, when all of her demons would come rushing out at her at once. And I'm still loyal to her to the point where I am not going to share what that was like. It was not pretty, I can tell you that.

For all the people who enjoyed DD in her touring persona and all of her so-called wild and free behaviour, I was the one keeping her alive so she could recover enough to go on the next adventure. And I can tell you that got just a little tiring sometimes, but I did it because I loved her and I knew she needed to do that, to live through that. That's why with these women who claim to have been with her … I have nothing to say to them. They're jealous because they know that I'm the love of DD's life. She was with me for the longest, and I set her free, but she always came back, and I know that she will come crawling back someday. I don't know if I'll be in a place where I wish to take her back, but I know that her destiny is to return to me, because I'm manifesting that.

AMY WILLIAMS

HER KITCHEN, FERNWOOD NEIGHBOURHOOD, VICTORIA, 2014

THAT EPIC TOUR WE DID. We were the Supersonic Grifters. We roamed the country from soup to nuts starting in Fernwood, Victoria, British Columbia, Canada, heading due east, all the way to goddamn Signal Hill, Newfoundland, a million thousand kilometres away, back west into Quebec for a while, then continued west and wound up in Calgary during the Folk Festival.

Yeah, we met Campbell Ouiniette there. He said he was gonna make us famous like the Low Johannahs, but then he disappeared. No, I wasn't there when they did the Stampede, that was later, that was a different tour, later. They kept the band name that I had helped come up with, but they *replaced* me with Giulietta on that one. Yeah. On my tour we were in Calgary during Folk Fest, not the Stampede. They're total opposites. Then we headed for home and finally imploded, or exploded, at the ferry terminal at Swartz Bay outside of Victoria again.

At first we let Jacob be in charge of the money. I don't know why we did that. I guess he was sort of our leader at first, anyway. Artistically? Or something? It's funny how you tend to give up leadership to anybody who just acts sure of themselves a lot. And Jacob always had that swagger to him. He always had an opinion, that's for sure. And he was very, very handsome back then. What a handsome, lovely boy he ruined. Himself.

So, we would get to a gas station, fill up, and then somebody would have to wake Jacob from his drunken unconsciousness and get him to reach into his duct-taped wallet and hand us some nasty, sweaty, wet bills. And always, always, he'd grumble about it. One time I remember him reaching into his unwashed pocket and saying, "This shit has got to stop." What the fuck does that even mean?

So after a while, I just started being the one to collect the money from the promoters, because I had a baby to feed. I mean, Wyatt was Jacob's baby, too, but that did not seem to be a major factor in Jacob's decision-making process.

I was in charge of the food money. We had two rules: nobody who's drinking whisky can drive, and nobody eats the baby food but the baby.

God, we were poor. So damn poor. I'm not rich now, but then, we would sometimes spend our mornings digging in our pockets to pool dimes and nickels, even pennies, to get something to eat. Some gigs only paid enough for gas in the van, to get us to a show that we were hoping would pay more than that. Sometimes we just stayed in a town because we had no money to move on. Because I was the mother, I somehow got nominated by default to be the responsible adult in the band. Looking back on it, my level of responsibility only existed in comparison with the others, who were basically living like stray dogs or something. DD had to remind Tom to take off his shoes at the end of the night. Then she'd have to stop him from pissing in them.

I'm proud that I was able to keep us all alive on a food budget of just over twenty bucks a day for five people. The baby's milk and a can of baby food came first and that was about five bucks a day. So, basically, most of the time you had to go to a Safeway or a Loblaws or a Sobeys and get the roast chicken. You got the roast chicken and a big bag of dinner rolls from the roll bin in the bakery department. We got our vitamin C from the bars we played, drinking screwdrivers, Caesars, and gin and tonics with a twist. So we never got scurvy like some bands we knew.

But really, if you wanted to feed five people, you had to go with the chicken. They have these roasted chickens in bags with aluminum on the inside. They're clearly the worst kind of battery hen, beak clipped off, whole-life-in-a-ten-inch-cage kind of birds, pumped full of God knows what kind of modern chemistry and hormones. I swear my left tit got bigger eating all that chicken. But it fed you. If you got some skin with the flesh, it tasted like something. Salt and pepper and grease, but it filled you up and gave you something do with your hands and mouth for ten minutes. And you wiped the grease from your hands on the inside of the roll and spread some free butter from the little pats at the deli counter on them.

We usually got at least a pizza or something from wherever we were playing, and most of the band was flying on speed or cocaine if we could get somebody to give us some, so that also saved on the food money because a lot of times people weren't hungry.

I think we were in Thunder Bay, and we'd just passed through what Rosalyn Knight calls the "great foodless region" of the Canadian Prairies. We'd had a lot of chicken by then. I admit that.

I was at the wheel and we pulled into the big parking lot of a Safeway on the outskirts of the city. We hadn't wanted to stay upstairs in the Royal Albert Hotel because it was so gross and Rosalyn had told us she'd found a dead body in the hallway there, so we'd left Winnipeg right after the show the night before, and it was probably getting toward noon and nobody'd eaten since a dinner of something really nasty at the Albert.

I put the Plush Monster in park and sighed, and began my short little song and dance of reaching into my pocket and shrugging and going, "Welp, I guess unless anybody has a better idea, I better go in and get the Universal Chicken," which is what we called it. Kind of like the "Universal Soldier" of the Buffy Sainte-Marie song.

That's when DD snapped. She grabbed the twenty out of my hand with a flick and a "gimme that," and climbed down onto the asphalt. She said, "I'm so *fucking sick* of eating *fucking chicken*," and stomped off toward the store.

We just lounged around waiting for her. I mean, I didn't *want* the job of feeding the fucking band. Just because I was a mother didn't mean I felt fucking nurturing toward everybody in the world, and I sure-as-shit wasn't feeling very nurturing toward the rest of the band after being jammed into a Ford Econoline with them for three weeks.

About five minutes later, DD comes out running. Under one arm, she's got a baguette and the biggest fucking wheel of cheese I've ever seen in my life. And she's booking it.

She jumps into the van, drops the cheese wheel once, leaps down to grab it, climbs back into the passenger chair, and yells, "Drive! Drive!" Meanwhile the biggest fuckin' butch-lookin' woman comes stalking out of the automatic doors of the Safeway. Not fat like roly-poly fat but fuckin' *built* like a fuckin' Scandinavian truck. She looked like if the giant fat lady from the opera did five years in maximum security and did a lot of weight training and took off her giant horned helmet and got a brush cut and put on a security-guard uniform.

And she was not in a hurry. She was determinedly heading right for us like an unstoppable force of the universe.

And DD yelled, "Drive! Drive! Fuckin' drive!" at me.

But it just wouldn't catch.

At this point we hadn't had the van for that long. We'd probably only put a couple thousand K on it so I think at that point it was normally starting. Later I did learn how to start a Ford Econoline by rolling it, but at this point it would normally have started. Still it was about a forty-two-year-old vehicle, so it didn't like to be rushed, if you know what I mean.

But fuckin' DD of course would never believe me that there was something wrong with the van. She would always blame my "girly driving" and have to look at the thing herself before she'd ever believe me about anything with a motor on it. So she reaches over and turns the key herself, and even lunges her foot over to the goddamn pedal to give it some gas — which, if I did that she'd be like, "Whoa! Don't flood the engine!" but she was clearly panicking.

Also it felt like the security-guard lady was somehow controlling the van with her mind, willing it to stay put. She didn't seem worried that we were gonna peel out and get away. It was like she *knew* the thing wasn't gonna start. She looked implacable. She looked like fucking *geography*, she was so solid.

It was summer so the windows were rolled all the way down. The van was built when probably only Cadillacs had AC. DD was still frantically trying to turn the ignition when the guard reached straight in, put her hand on DD's shoulder, and said, "You. You're coming with me."

I was like *holy shit*. This is some serious trouble we've got ourselves into here. And DD obviously was thinking the same. She kind of gulped and meekly climbed down out of the van. I've rarely, if ever, seen her look so much at a loss.

The security guard took a look in the van, which was a mess of wrappers and magazines and musical equipment and shit, plus little Wyatt sleeping behind me in his car seat strapped into the first bench, and the rest of the band with their electrician-taped glasses and jean jackets with punk-band logos in felt pen and crumpled hats, lacking every kind of personal hygiene habit known to man. Anyway, the guard did a visual sweep of the van, raised her eyebrows when she saw the baby, then grabbed DD and walked her back into the store, carrying the baguette and the giant wheel of cheese. We didn't say shit. We just watched her go.

About twenty minutes goes by, and we're starting to wonder what the fuck we should do. Tom is like, "Well, looks like we're gonna be fuckin' buskin' for bail money in downtown Thunder Bay."

But then DD comes waltzing out, carrying the cheese and the bread, *plus* a giant, four-litre jug of milk, a pack of forty size-2

Huggies, a huge deli tray of cut vegetables, and God knows what else. You can't see much of her face with all the shit she's carrying, but she's got a lit smoke in her mouth that's sending up a cheerful cloud. The butch security lady is just watching from the doorway with her arms folded, no discernible expression on her face.

I'm like, "What the fuck, DD?"

She exhales smoke and says, "I'm banned for life from Safeway."

As we're merging onto the highway, I have to ask, "What did you do?" DD says nothing.

"Did you do her?" I just ask to be mischievous. She turns and raises her eyebrows, smirking.

"Wouldn't *you* like to know."

I think she probably just cried at her. But you could never be sure with DD.

MIRUNA MOLNAR

HER HOME, GALIANO ISLAND, B.C., 2016

I HAVE A THEORY ABOUT DD that, no matter what, she'll always be a runaway at heart.

I had never been to Galiano, but I'd been to Salt Spring Island, and I was really into, you know, being in nature and the water and the trees and everything. And I was fully in love with her, body and soul. Sometimes I would think she was the wisest, most magical person, but even at the start there were inklings that something was a bit off, missing … the wiring was funny. But when you're in love, any inklings tend to go by the wayside. My heart was pounding, my hands were clammy. I was so nervous when I got off the ferry, I hardly noticed the Douglas firs, the eagles, all of that, except as being … being a part of my feelings of excitement for new life, new love. It was as wonderful then as it became awful later.

She came to meet me on her motorcycle. I'd never ridden a motorcycle before. She gave me her patented heart-melting look of happiness, and said, "You're here! Yippee!" and that made me feel a sudden warmth — it made me somewhat nervous and afraid, but also, really good. Then she had a thought. "Oh dear, I only have the one helmet. I should've borrowed another one to pick you up with." But she didn't seem that upset that she had to go without one and let the wind blow through her mohawk. I remember her hair was completely buzzed to the skin on either side. I put on the helmet, she helped me climb on behind her, and I put my arms around her and leaned in. It truly was a delicious, sweet feeling as we started to rumble away.

Right then I heard her say, "Oh shit — cops." I looked to the left and saw the Mountie in his cruiser off on a side road start to move. I could see that he saw us, and DD saw that, too, so she shouted, "Hold on tight!" and she gunned the motor. We took off so fast you wouldn't believe it. Motorcycles seem to be able to get going fast, faster than a car, if you see what I'm talking about. They accelerate. So we accelerated out of there on this suddenly howling, moaning, beast of a machine, and I had to use all the strength in my body to hold onto her in a panic and she just whizzed us over that undulating island road. At first I was completely blown out on the sensory overload of speeding on a motorcycle for the first time in my life. When I had a minute to get used to that, I thought, *Wow, this person is really exciting!* But then after another minute or so it crossed my mind, *Umm, what are we doing? Running away from the cops? Isn't this an island? Is there something I don't know? Maybe we're going to hide in the woods or something?* But after a few more minutes we pulled up in front of her little rented house, which was going to be our little rented house, and we dismounted, and I didn't say anything because I really wasn't sure what to say.

She brought me in and offered me tea, and as the kettle was beginning to boil, sure enough, the cop pulled into the driveway, because he knew DD, of course, like everyone else on the island. I said, "Uh, the police are here." She kind of sighed and said, "Oh, boy. I'm not sure what I was thinking there." And she walked out to have a chat with Mike the cop.

So, that was an inkling there, where for no reason except an instinct to run away from authority or something, she kind of switched into flight mode and did this bizarre high-speed chase to nowhere.

Of course, she smoothed it over with Mike the cop somehow, charmed him. Not that he was mad at her, but mostly just baffled, like me. He liked her. I think she had even taught Mike's kid violin. Later, in bed, she told me that it was her old dad who'd ingrained in her the instinct to, you know, step on it if the cops were after you, and that he was always outrunning them out on the logging roads on Vancouver Island. I thought, *Jeez, what kind of parent teaches their kid to burn rubber when they see a policeman?* (Later, I did meet old Dad and I wouldn't put it past him, that's for sure.) But that was kind of ... weird. I forgot about it after a while, but later it came back to me. She is so much stranger than most people know. I really thought I could handle it. But I guess I really couldn't. Or I really shouldn't have told myself that I ought to be able to handle it.

CARLA PATTERSON

HER STRIP BAR, PORT ——, 2015

YEAH, DD COMES HERE SOMETIMES, but not in a long time. I don't know when was the last time.

Yeah, she was my first real friend. Maybe ever. I was out in the hall, where the teacher liked to put my desk, first year of junior high. I saw her get kicked out of her classroom a few doors down. She was walking in my direction toward the principal's office. She grabbed one of those heating pipes that run along the ceiling and did a flip over it. Then she winked at me, and when she got to my desk, she whispered, "Hey, can you hold these for me? Case they search me?" and handed me off a little baggie of pills. "Go ahead and take one if you want." Ha. I was high for two full days.

No, yeah, she came to this place a lot. DD likes a good tittie bar. And this is my place. I own it. I actually won it in a fucking epic poker game eleven years ago. It was kind of like hitting the jackpot and kind of like having a curse put on your life. I try to make it a good thing. It's a strip bar, but in a way it's also a community centre, but with more cash and cocaine swirling around. I demand that the boys respect the women who dance here, and if they don't, I have them thrown out or I throw them out myself. I'm a big girl, and I don't take shit from anybody in my bar. They try to touch my girls, they get thrown out. They talk disrespect to my girls, call them skank hos or whatever, they get thrown out. They try to fight in here, we put the hurt on 'em. Simple as that. Take it outside. And if they start beating the shit out of each other in the parking lot, I don't mind calling the cops, 'cause I know the cops here *real* well, and I know I'm not ratting anybody out because they're just going to break it up with their nightsticks and nobody is going to lay any charges. I have figured out a working relationship with the boys in blue. You know what I mean. Enough said.

The thing is, the cops, the drunk jerks at the bar, the peelers, and the crazy chicks that flash their tits for free at the end of the night, I know them all. They're all the people who yelled "fuckin' dirty Indians" at me and DD in the schoolyard, they're the ones who wouldn't talk to us or invite us to their parties in junior high, they're the ones who would talk behind my back, who would call me and DD "nasty fucking lesbo dykes."

But this is my bar. I won this bar because I was smarter than them, because I understand the pure mathematics of how to play poker, despite the fact that I was put in the hallway every math class. Their world is about who owns what, and I own the place. The deed is in my name. And I run the place. And they know it's something they couldn't do. I have their respect because I took their stuff and I own it by their own insane rules. And I can handle myself in the world of drunk horny craziness wayyy better than any of them, believe me. Funny enough, I protect them. Bad shit can happen in a strip club, in any bar, and I do a pretty decent job of keeping fights to a minimum, and keeping young ladies from going home with gentlemen when they're too wasted to know what's happening. Do I get thanked for that? No. Usually it's like, "Fuck you, big fat Indian bitch. Mind your own fucken business." But that's where I've got them. This here *is* my business. And the peeler girls like working here, 'cause unlike most places, they don't have to suck the manager's dick to get enough shifts to feed their babies.

The way it works is, there's a pattern to the evening. First there's the after-work crowd, men who come to have a beer, watch the girls dance, maybe watch an eastern hockey game on the TVs at the same time. If DD's in town, she'll come by before the game and start drinking Kokanee even before the after-work crowd, because she's been visiting her mom and she can only take so much of the day with her before she's had enough and she needs a beer. By about six thirty the married men who wanna stay married start going home for supper. But some of the men decide to really get their drink on and stay, and they order the burger-and-beer special.

Then after dinner, the couples start to come in to get the burger-and-beer deal, and then after that, the clumps of single girls and dudes come in. Everybody knows everybody and everybody has bumped uglies with everybody at one time or another, but at this point early in the evening, things are pretty casual. The professionals dance, and people talk shit about their boss or their day or whatever. That's when DD and me catch up, talk about what's been goin' on. She'll say she's in town for a week but I know she's probably gonna be gone in a couple days 'cause her mom is gonna piss her off too much.

The stripping and the quiet drinking goes on for a couple of hours and then things start to ramp up. At ten thirty, the professional girls take a break and the dance floor opens up. At first it's just the regular single girls dancing with each other to Beyoncé or whatever. Then the girls who are in a relationship drag their boyfriends out on the dance floor. The boyfriends do that thing where they look off somewhere and pretend they haven't noticed a pretty girl is yanking on their arm, and then when they do stand up they kind of look around, embarrassed, to see if anybody's watching. Then it slowly dawns on them that if they want to get sex tonight they better dance, and they start to move. Most of them are the fucking shittiest dancers, like clunky robots, but the younger guys are a little better dancers these days, their bums are a little looser like maybe they let their woman finger their ass. Some of them are already pretty lovey-dovey by eleven. I like it when DD's here because we can kinda watch and laugh at them together. She calls them breeders.

After an hour of dancing, we get the strippers out again, and that's when the single and sort-of-single guys who've been scoping the room out start to make their moves and start chatting up the prospects. They chat about this or that and usually either get shot down hard or just given a signal of no interest, which they may or may not be too drunk already to read.

Then the strippers take another break and the dance floor really comes alive. The dudes are making their moves, and some girls will go out to dance with them. Everybody's been pretending it had no effect on them to have these hard-bodied chicks with pierced clits rolling around on the stage, sometimes together, sometimes just solo with their legs apart, but it's been having its effect, with the booze, and people are just pretty damn horny, and they start making out a little on the dance floor.

Then about a half hour after midnight, the strippers come out and strip on the stage with the regular dance floor going at the same time. That's when things start to go crazy, Port-style. The shooters — Sex on the Beach, Irish Car Bomb, tequila-and-Sprite slammers — they start to fly back and whack down on the bar, the dancing gets sloppy, the men move their hands up then down to the girls' asses, and grind. The cocaine, which was being done quietly in the can, is now out on the table. What about the cops? Yeah, sometimes just maybe certain cops might be there, doing their share, with a girl rubbing their arm. That's how it is.

Then when it gets late it can really get wild. I've seen girls giving head at the tables, on the dance floor, getting dry humped up against the jukebox. Occasionally strippers but it's mostly civilians. Beer is spilling, the music's pumping, the songs switch from slinky R&B to hard rock. AC/DC. Guns N' Roses. Iron Maiden.

That's when I have to be really alert. It's not out of the question that I might do a bump or two myself at this point 'cause I have to stay on my toes. Looking out for what me and DD call the Angry Bear.

Booze is a creature. It's a product of fucking yeast. Yeast is an animal. And when you're going hard, you're living in what science calls symbiosis with this booze creature. It's a demon. And if the demon is in a bad mood, it will just jump in and take possession of somebody. Man or woman. And the demon wants to fuck. It wants something to fuck. And if it looks around and there's nobody who wants to fuck, the booze creature makes some calculations. Maybe somebody can be tricked into fucking. But if the booze creature looks around, and looks in the mirror, and sees that nobody is gonna wanna fuck this human it's possessing, well, then the creature gets fucken angry. And then all kinds of hurricane mayhem starts to happen, and I don't want that in my bar.

There's a kind of walk that a man will do when he's got the Angry Bear in him. His footfalls are super hard on the floor. He plants each step with a slow deliberation, like he's fucking killing a rat with his heavy foot every time he steps. He orders a shot and he knocks it back and he *slams* it down on the bar. He drinks a beer and then he *slams* it down. He's scanning the room. He's watching these people having a crazy good time and he sees through it all. Those women are all sluts and whores and those shitheads who are having all the luck with them might think they're hot shit but they ain't so tough. No, they ain't so tough. Probably go down with one punch, unlike him who could take a beating and get back up and come at them again to the bitter end of the fight.

I see those guys right away. I send my boys over to talk to them. I've got them trained. They have a few techniques but the best way is to kind of trick them a little bit. What they do is they go over there and say, "Hey, man. How's it lookin' out there?" and usually the Angry Bear says nothing because he's not really in the talking mode, and that's part of the idea of talking with them, in a friendly way, is to wake up the people-creature trapped in there with the yeast demon. I have my boy say, "Hey, so listen, you're obviously someone who can handle themselves. See anybody out there who looks like they could be the fighting type?" and the Angry Bear kind of has to look at the room in a new way, a way that asks if anybody in the bar might be a danger to others. Which is not how the Bear has been thinking about the bar. Then my boy says something like, "Listen, it's getting pretty crazy in here. If somebody starts any trouble, can I count on you for help if I need to bum-rush some asshole outta here? I could use a spare pair of hands, sometimes."

Pretty much always, the Bear will nod and let the bouncer know he's got his back, that he's on board for the project of keeping the peace in the bar.

With the chicks it's way harder. Chicks are way better at hiding their true emotions, so they can be all smiley-smiley, "Great to see you, hon! Looove your hair! Looove that dress!" and then a second later they turn around with a broken glass in their hand and they're like, "I'll fucken cut yer face you stupid fucken cum-sucking bitch." And then there's no fucken solution except to get three bouncers to grab her, get her arms, get her legs, and lock her in a car I keep on blocks in the back just for that sole purpose, till she calms down or passes out in there. Then you see some whacked-out shit. They kick and scream and rip around in that old Chrysler New Yorker, steaming up the windows with their sweat and their hate. That's when you know it's truly a possession. What a great gift the White Man brought us when he brought booze to this country. Fuck.

Yeah, then we come to the so-called end of the night, which is not the end of the night for me, but for the amateurs. The smart operators know that fifteen minutes before last call gets announced they gotta find somebody fast, and if they're horny enough they're pretty fucking shameless about making their play for some of that pussy. And you bet the standards drop. It's all pretty fucked up. Everybody knows about closing time. I don't have to explain that.

Then the bell rings, and we start to bring up the lights, but not all the way, 'cause that's a little too harsh, and the youngest doorman has the job of shouting, "All right, folks, we're closed now. You don't have to go home but you can't stay here. So let's *clear out*!"

And we gradually, but not slowly, herd the people out of the bar, except for the people we really want to be there. Then we lock the doors and bring down the shades. And once I count the cash and put it in the safe, I actually get to relax a little.

That's when *my* party starts. Although lately I go home sooner than I used to. But those were good times, a few years back now, with DD and the lock-in dance parties. I'll let the bouncers stay, if they want, but not if they ain't gonna dance. Unless a guy is pretty special, it's mostly all-girl lock-in. Like if the whole bar was the girls' can.

It's especially fun for me and DD, 'cause, you know, we go so far back, to when it was just her and me against the world. I went with her when she ran away from home, when her mom decided she was devil spawn and was ready to beat the gay outta her, and we wound up in Ucluelet at this campground called Big Woody, renting the space under a picnic table for fifteen bucks a night. When she's here in my place, and it's open bar 'cause it's my fucken bar and we're hitting it, it's like, you know, you've come a long way, baby! Yeah.

The strippers all love DD. And it sure is funny how somehow, somewhere in there, one of them always seems to get the idea of having DD do coke off her tits, and it's always a different girl, and the girl always thinks it was somehow *her* idea. And DD's always like, "Who, me? Oh, dear," like she's trying to resist the idea. That girl is tricky. She's trick-*ee*. Don't think you're gonna find her.

NAME WITHHELD

BELFAST, 2013

THE SECOND THING I NOTICED ABOUT HER was that she was sitting at a table, laughing and drinking, with some of the hardest-looking men I've ever seen in my life. I mean, serious, serious-looking people. It was Donnacha McKeague's bar, so there would sometimes be fellows such as them in it, although they always behaved themselves when they were there. They had too much respect for him to settle their differences or deal with business in his place. There's a skill, or possibly truly a matrix of skills, one might say, to running a proper bar, and the McKeagues have been doing it for at least six generations.

I've heard the story told on more than one occasion that when Donnacha had to leave the other bar he was running, it was because the police found a cache of weapons in a hidden storeroom. They say when he was setting up his next bar, the Miscellaneous, some masked men came in with knives to rob the place. They say that he reached for the phone to hit a speed-dial button. The men shouted gruffly, "You call the police and you're dead!" And they say that yer man responded quietly, cool as you like, "Oh, I'm not phonin' the police, boys," and fixed the leader in the eyes with a steady look. The leader said, "Oh," dropped his knife on the floor, and said, "Oh, fucking jeezus, we didn't mean it, we didn't know." And him, who is known for always being ready with a quick wit, said, "There's a lot you don't know, boy. If you clear out right now, maybe you won't have to learn it all today," and they apologized again and left.

Now there was DD, sitting and laughing with these big, hard men, who were also laughing. They had big wide grins on their faces. There was three or four of them. They all had broken noses and were absolutely twice her size in every direction. Still they were treating her like one of their own, or perhaps more like they'd found a small, rare creature of myth and legend. They were literally delighted with her, these giant scary men whooping it up with this little lesbian with teeth missing on either side of her incisors that made her look like she had fangs. I swear I've never seen anything like it. After they did a round of shots of tequila, I saw her poke one in the belly button with her index finger, this gorilla of a man with tattoos of a distinctly republican nature, and he giggled like a little girl, so he did, no word of a lie.

Obviously I was sort of watching it all out of the corner of my eye. I was at the bar, reading my book. I remember I was reading a translation of a Basque poet I'd never heard of. It was quite good but I don't remember who it was. I was supposed to be meeting some friends there later.

I was watching her out of the corner of my eye, and, as I was after telling you, I thought I could tell certain things about her that perhaps others would not. And then I noticed that she was watching *me* out of the corner of *her* eye.

She got up from the table and made some comment to the men, and they all roared and pounded the table and held their sides, and she sort of hopped in the direction of the bog, leaving them laughing, taking the subtlest sidelong glance in my direction. I knew that she knew that I knew she was communicating with me.

She was in the bog for quite some time. When she came out she came to the bar. She called to the huge boys in the back, "I think that it is my *SHOUT*, people! Is that the word you people use when you buy the drinks here? You *SHOUT*!?"

"*YES!*" shouts one of them. "*THAT'S VERY CULTURALLY SENSITIVE OF YOU THERE, DD!*"

So DD playfully *SHOUT*s her drink order at McKeague, who pretends that he doesn't hear her shouting, and could she shout any louder, please, and DD obliges him, and she's standing beside me as he pours the drinks. And she turns to me and says quietly, "I need to get away from these guys. Can you help?"

I nodded.

"Are you ready to leave pretty much now?"

I nodded again. "I know somewhere safe we can go."

Her head tilted slightly, querulously, when I said the word *safe*, in a communication that was a shared ironic understanding of the word. Of how often it is used and how often it's a lie. But I held her gaze, letting her know that I did consider where we were going to be a safe place, or as safe as one could reasonably expect in this world, the rape world, which is the true world that we do, in fact, live in … which is rarely spoken of in the newspapers or in polite society. Does that make you nervous? I can't help but notice you're picking at your fingers.

DD says quietly, "I'm going to go tell them I'm leaving with you, and then we'll go? Is that okay with you?"

I looked her directly in the eye. "Yes. I'm ready to go."

"Do you want a tray?" Donnacha had the round of beer and shots in front of her.

She switched back into her party voice. "Fuck no! I got this!"

She carried all of it back to the table, so she did, like a professional barmaid, and they cheered her return. They threw back the shots together, and then she said something quietly to them, with an exaggerated mock-innocent-not-innocent look on her face, then motioned with a mock-discrete-not-discrete head nod over to me at the bar. A rising, deep-voiced "Whoa, DD!!" rose up from the table, and the men all raised their pints to her. She did a little bow, picked up her fiddle case, drank her Guinness in one long go, belched so loud I could hear it clear across the busy bar, and did another little bow as the men cheered. She hugged each of the men in turn, with real warmth, and traipsed back toward the bar, toward me, as the big hard men cheered, "Aaay, DD!!!" And we were on our way out the door.

As we walked down the street, she took a couple of quick glances behind her. "Did you tell them you'd pulled me?" I knew she had.

"What?"

"Did you tell them you'd pulled?"

"Oh. Right. Yes, sorry. It's the only way guys like that let you leave the group. If you're scoring."

I knew that was right.

"It's okay. Come on. Let's get on this bus. I'll take you to my place."

MYKOLA LOYCHUCK

GREEN ROOM AREA, RUDOLSTADT-FESTIVAL, RUDOLSTADT, GERMANY, 2015

THERE IS A STATE OF BEING THAT HAPPENS to you after you've been playing with DD for a while, and then you're not playing with her anymore. It's kind of like what Murakami said in *A Wild Sheep Chase* — there's this sheep that has a star on it and if you find it and it enters your being, but then it leaves you, then you enter the state of being *sheepless*. You're bereft and you can't really function so good anymore, because all you do all day is just hang around thinking about how you wish that you had the sheep with the star on its head inside your mind but you don't anymore. It can be that way with DD.

Because playing with DD draws out the best aspects of your playing, especially live, where you're connecting with her, and you're connecting with how you're feeling right now, and ... and you're also doing that with everybody else who you're playing with, and importantly, that includes everybody who is listening, everyone in the audience.

Because the fundamental thing about music is, the thing is, it's ... I know how this sounds, sorry but it's a form of magic, a form of telekinesis, because no matter what you're playing, no matter who you're playing to, if ... if you have complete and utter faith that the thing that you are feeling will be transmitted to the other people in the room, then that feeling really will be transmitted.

You can't fake it, you can't pretend to yourself that you are really feeling something, and then have that feeling come across. *You* know, right? I know that you do.

It's extremely hard to focus and stay in that place. The process of playing a song is really the process of wandering through the chords and the words and the melody like you're wandering in a forest, and you're hunting for these split-second moments where the feeling actually happens. And just like an old-fashioned animal hunter, there's times when you go out there with your rifle and you come home with the bag empty.

When you play with DD, she is hunting with you, like a hunting guide through your own song, and ... and she's really good at it, and you catch a lot more of those moments.

But it's easy to stop thinking of DD as a co-hunter, and start thinking of her as a magic bullet. I mean, like in that musical William Burroughs wrote with Tom Waits, where he says you tell yourself that you'll save the magic bullets just for your bad days, but then soon enough every day without the magic bullets is a bad day. Like that. Dependent. You grow dependent. You think, *I don't know where I am with this song, but I know if I throw to DD she's gonna whip off something amazing, so let's just ride through until we get there.* And that's no good. That is not a good idea.

For example, I remember we played the Edge of the World Festival up in Haida Gwaii, and the moment she landed, DD was totally entranced with the place, looking around at all the greenness and natural scenery. We went to the bar and we started drinking, and she said, "Our concert's not till Sunday, right?" and I said yeah, and I went to the can. And then she was just gone. I spent all Friday night, all Saturday day, all Sunday day wondering what the fuck happened to DD. There I was in what's supposedly one of the most beautiful places on Earth, and all I could think of is "where the fuck is DD?" and I was perhaps freaking out that I was going to have to go on without her. And I realized that I'd come to lean on her waaay too much. I had to sit down and have a talk with myself, where I just said, "Look, DD found you to play with, right? So, you must be good enough to do this without her. Right? Besides, she'll probably be back in time, because she always is, right?" I realized I was letting myself get a little too far into the DD-ness of playing, and I had to sort my head out a bit, which is something I … something I try to do sometimes. Something I have to do often.

Then, of course, she came waltzing up to the stage at ten minutes to showtime with a big grin on her face. It took everything in me not to say, "Where the fuck were you, you little shit!" because what's the point of that, and what would it have got me except less DD instead of more. And of course she played fucking fantastic, and I did okay, too, I think … I hope.

But not everybody is as strong as that when they get used to hunting for those moments with DD. For some people, when she's gone, they starve. They just starve.

AMY WILLIAMS

HER KITCHEN, FERNWOOD NEIGHBOURHOOD, VICTORIA, 2014

I DIDN'T REALLY COME DOWN WITH postpartum depression until the new band went on tour without me. Can you get postpartum depression when a baby is fourteen months old? I guess it was more like post-Parton depression. Post–Dolly Parton's "Jolene." That "Jolene" was our standby when we were busking across the country. It was our standby song. I know it's been overplayed since then, but I never got tired of it and I never will. That was one of the ways that me and DD first connected, because we both agreed Dolly Parton was a fucking genius. Which she is. That's probably a less ludicrous-sounding thing to say now, when her image is more of a legendary scrappy survivor and all, but not too long ago, she was mostly just a punchline for big-breast jokes on the *Tonight Show*. But I said, "Dolly Parton is a poet and a fucking genius" at Rosalyn Knight's Hullaballoo Open Mic at Tuesday's, and DD was like, "Amen, sister!" and we clinked glasses. I don't know if we'd even met formally at that point. But we agreed about that.

When she played "Jolene" with you, she was exquisite. I mean, just setting aside the way her violin seemed like it was made to blend with my old pawnshop, no-name guitar. No, I mean, on "Jolene," we were something. She never played it the same way twice. You would sing that rising "Jolene, Jo-*lene,* Jolene, *Jole-e-e-ene*!" and she would ride the chords low and quiet as you sang it up, and then as you held that last "*e-e-e-ene*!" part she'd slide on in and make her high comment on how she felt about the subject of jealousy on this particular day.

Sometimes it would be something beautiful and wounded, like, "how could you do this to me, my one true love Jolene?" and sometimes it would be a loud nasty *scrrraawwnk* that was just like, "fu-u-u-uck you, you no-good home wrecker bitch fucking Jolene." Or it could be a high tormented scream, or a mid-range kind of "can we talk about this like reasonable people, instead of overgrown children, for goodness sake, Jolene?" All of these things or none or more would be her comment on the song, always making the song mean something else. It was a pleasure to play "Jolene" with her. One of the greatest pleasures of my life.

And when they left, leaving me to stay home with Wyatt, I can honestly say that my heart was truly broken.

I wasn't *with* DD at the time, although we'd already messed around a lot by then. I was officially with Jacob, that fucking jerk. But it wasn't him leaving or even DD leaving that killed me. It was the *band* leaving, *my band* leaving town without me to go on untold adventures and suffer and triumph and be disrespected and play gloriously and play shitty and sing with a ratched-out voice from too much travel and no sleep and be utterly unable to know what to do with a broken transmission by the side of the road fifty clicks outside of Lloydminster on the Saskatchewan side where the road gets bumpier … and all that stuff. I was out of it. My band was going out there, and I was staying home to be a *single-mother housewife*. Motherfuck. You know?

I'd asked my goddamn mother to watch Wyatt while I went on the road, but she folded her arms and told me that if I intended to live that way, I could go all right, but I would have to sign some papers so that Wyatt wouldn't have to deal with this kind of instability in his life. I saw how the land was lying there, that fucking woman, my mother.

Those were the choices, then. Be who I wanted to be, be who I really was, and lose my baby — or keep my baby. I will never burden my kid with the thought that somehow *if it wasn't for him, blah blah blah*, but Jesus fucking Christ it fucking hurt like hell to see that stupid Ford Econoline putter out of the driveway on its way to the ferry terminal. It fucking *killed.*

And that's why I don't play any songs about how fucking tough the lonely road is for us musicians. Not even the well-written ones. Partly because those songs are just tricked-out come-ons — "Oh, I'm so darn lonely, won't you help me make it through the night by sucking my dick, baby?" But also because I fucking *know* there's so many fucking women musicians who would have *loved* to have had that experience of the so-called lonely road in their twenties and thirties but had to fucking get *off* the *lonely fucking road* because the father was sure-as-shit not going to be the one staying home to watch the baby and there was nobody else stepping up either. Rock-star girls with major-label deals might get the rock 'n' roll nanny paid for, but even some of *them* get dropped like a brick when they get knocked up. It's just too much trouble. Too much trouble. That's what I became. I refuse to be bitter about it, because I will never regret holding on to my Wyatt and I learned a lot of wisdom that a lot of people are fucking bereft of, and I'm not sorry, and I'm not bitter … but fuck, it fucking killed me when my band went back out on the road without me. You can play "Jolene" alone in your kitchen all you want, but "Jolene" means something else again when you're playing it in your kitchen and your band is out there heading toward Montreal without you.

GIULIETTA CAETANO

HER HOUSE, TUCSON, ARIZONA, 2016

OH, MAN! TOURING WITH DD BACK THEN was so much fun! I was brought in as a replacement for Amy. I think I met her once or twice at the Hullaballoo Open Mic there in Vic. I didn't know her. Of course DD was sad Amy wasn't coming but what can you do? You gotta make the best of it, make the music happen, man. Touring can be hell on Earth. But not with DD. Not back then, anyway. She always made it fun. Just hanging around in the back of the van smoking was a good time. We had a lot of laughs.

I hadn't toured too much at that point, so DD was kind of my, like, tour mentor. Which was great 'cause nothing seemed to phase her. Of course, there was all the dos and don'ts, like don't sleep with your shoes on, don't miss an opportunity to piss, never go for sushi or order espresso on the prairies. But the key she understood was that you gotta find little goofball ways to have fun while you're between one town and another, 'specially if it's five hundred miles to the next gig.

She introduced me to the two games I still find myself playing when I'm out there on the highways and the byways: *Anal RV* and *Whitesnake*. I don't know where she learned them from.

Anal RV is pretty simple: you just see a recreational vehicle out on the road (and you get stuck behind a lot of them) and you just add the word *anal* to the name of it. It's super fun 'cause RVs in North America in particular seem to have names that, um, I dunno, evoke a kind of messed-up relationship with Nature-with-a-capital-N. Sometimes it would be adversarial, and sometimes it would be admiring, almost mystical. So, it's pretty fun to put the word *anal* in front of that. For immature people like us, anyhow.

Anal Adventurer. Anal Frontier. Anal Vanguard. Anal Cougar. Anal Mystique (oooh ...). Anal Comfort (aaah ...). Anal Journey. Anal Bigfoot. (That one, for some reason, always put in my head this image of, like, a real neat and tidy giant hairy metrosexual sasquatch, livin' in a Japanese minimalist-style apartment, and you know, like, his socks are folded and ordered by colour.)

Anal Conqueror. Anal HitchHiker. Anal HitchHiker is real good, but what about Anal HitchHiker II? Twice as good, man. Anal Ranger. Anal Prowler (look out!). Anal Vengeance (yikes!). Anal Dutchman. "Uh-oh, here comes the Anal Dutchman." "Why do they call you Anal Dutchman, Mister Van Gogh?"

We all had our favourites for sure. For myself, the greatest moment of that game was on the way out of Nelson, when we passed an RV called ... Leprechaun. That was the winner for me and DD.

The other game, *Whitesnake*, is, I think, a little more, uh, elegant, because you don't have to add a word to anything, you just make a mental link, like internally. It all happens in your head. All it is, what you do, is you think of a band name. Go ahead — think of a band name. Hold it in your mind. Got it? Don't tell me, just hold it there. Okay.

Now think of that band name as a way to describe ... a bowel movement. A way to tell somebody about a shit you took. Right? Oh yeah, you toured with DD — you must've played *Whitesnake.*

What were some of my faves? Well, Whitesnake, of course. And the classics, like the Rolling Stones, and Yes. The Cure. The Clash. And you could really get a lot out of the bands with colours in their names. Deep Purple. Black Sabbath. Simply Red. I like Simply Red.

Anal RV was more of a strict road game. You'd have to actually see the RV before you could call it out, and you had to be alert, but you really felt this total surge of adrenalin if you were the first to point and shout, "Anal Slingshot! P'twaaang!" Sometimes we would relax the rules and allow for cars to be in the game. The Fords were good. Ford Focus. Ford Explorer. Ford Escape. Ford Probe, naturally.

But see, *Whitesnake* would occasionally take over your life, up into the time of the gig itself, because you'd walk into the club and there'd be all these band posters and all you'd be thinking of while the sound guy was talking to you was how to think of some band to top DD with in *Whitesnake*, and it would sneak into your conversation out of nowhere. You'd be talking about how many DIs the band needed and find yourself suddenly shouting, "Wham!" or "Old Crow Medicine Show!" or "Dexys Midnight Runners!" Then she'd fire back from across the bar: "Midnight Oil! Ewww!"

Even now, on tour solo, I wind up just running those games in my mind, to keep myself amused. 'Specially in Europe, where there's always new band names and new van names to be discovered. I almost called DD up a while ago when I was in Augsburg and I saw a little camper van called a Nugget. But I didn't.

NAME WITHHELD

BELFAST, 2013

SHE SAID SHE WASN'T EVER AFRAID for her safety from the big burly men with the republican tattoos. Which was what I had assumed. "No, they were great guys, true gentlemen," she assured me.

She told me she was meeting up with her band in two days to do the artist-in-residence gig at this arts festival that takes place right in Belfast that I hadn't even known about but was apparently in its fourth year. Belfast can be like that. Her band was some kind of Ukrainian music or something, though she could also play a number of tunes from here quite well.

She told me she'd decided to come two weeks early to check out Ireland, and had immediately started playing on the street upon landing at Shannon. She'd found Dublin to be "kinda boring" and had taken a bus to Galway, which she also characterized, I recall, as more touristy than she expected. She said it was "like going to Irelandland." She sounded a bit disappointed with Ireland. She said she'd imagined that Ireland would look green and lush with moss on everything everywhere like a King Arthur film. I said that's an English story but we both agreed that England didn't look like that either. We both agreed that England was a shithole. She said there was a place in Canada, far, far to the west, on the edge of the world, that did look like that, like a King Arthur legend, but I don't recall whether she said the name of it, except I remember her saying it was at the edge of the world. That struck me as a poetic way to describe a place. I asked if she'd been to the Giant's Causeway and she said no.

She'd slept above a pub in Galway after sitting in on a late-night session, and stayed on with some Italian students from the university. Then she'd gotten bored with that and went out onto the highway to hitchhike. I've never hitched a ride alone in a foreign country but she told me that Canadians do this all the time, even small women alone.

So, the first ride she gets is these hard men in a van, the ones I saw her with in the pub. They said they picked her up because they had business plans for the future, in which good luck would be an asset, and the driver's personal superstition was that it was good luck to be giving a musician a ride, and they'd seen her fiddle case. They asked her to give them a tune as they drove and she said she "busted out some crazy Romanian shit" and they just loved it. They decided to adopt her. They took her all the way to the North, to Belfast, to their local, where they bought her endless Guinness and showed her how it was supposed to be poured and how it was supposed to be properly enjoyed. She said they were impressed with how much she could drink and impressed that after all the beer she could still beat them at pool, although they argued about the rules. I asked her if they were from Belfast and she said that they'd told her they were all originally from Derry. I said, "I suppose they all said they were from Derry and none of them said they were from Londonderry," and she said, "Where's Londonderry?" and I said, "Right."

They lived in a "crappy little house in some poor suburbs" but she said that none of them owned it. She asked them if they were on holiday, since they never went to work but just lifted weights on a 1970s weightlifting bench and watched television and ate bacon and eggs and soda bread all day and drank at the pub one block away in the evening. They said they were "not exactly on holiday but 'sort of, in a manner of speaking' being freelance builders waiting for the next job contract." She noticed that Michael, the eldest of the group, under no circumstances would he ever actually leave the house at all, but he would say, "You lads enjoy yourselves at the pub, there's a match on later that I don't want to miss." But sometimes the younger "lads" would be sent out on an errand, and they would say, "DD, can you play us one of your crazy Romanian tunes for luck before I'm off to do my errand?" and the fellows would close their eyes and lean against something and listen so intently she felt like they were soaking the music up "like very dry sponges."

In fact, she said she was quite happy to be in their little neighbourhood for a week or so where she got to know some of the kids in that row of houses, and even gave a couple of piano lessons, and the beer at the pub was especially good and Michael would tell folk stories about the Four Treasures, and everything would have been fine. However.

Being polite, the men liked to hear more about DD and her life back in Canada than to talk about themselves. They were very polite men.

But they would ask, "How is the beer in Canada, then? Not as good, eh? Does it taste like piss, like American beer?" Or, "So, is it the same in Canada that if you want the bus to come, you light a smoke?" or what have you. Unfortunately after eight or ten pints DD made mention of some friends she'd had who rode motorcycles on Vancouver Island, and that led her to let slip that some of them were members of the Satan's Angels motorcycle club — or the Hells Angels? The Hells Angels, that's right. She said that when she let that out, right away she knew she'd made a mistake, because all the boys became very interested in that, especially old Michael, who wanted to know if DD's friends carried protection for themselves. DD joked, "Nah, they don't ever use condoms," and everyone laughed, and then Michael later slowly but reliably worked the talk around to asking about her friends over on Vancouver Island and where they might be getting their weapons and ammunition. Michael was wondering if DD still remembered any phone numbers of any of those old friends, and DD was feeling a bit uncomfortable about how this was all going. *That* was the reason she had to give her new friends the slip when they went into Donnacha McKeague's bar.

MYKOLA LOYCHUCK

GREEN ROOM AREA, RUDOLSTADT-FESTIVAL, RUDOLSTADT, GERMANY, 2015

THE *FIRST* TIME I PLAYED WITH HER? ... I had gone down to the Railway Club to see Rosalyn Knight, and DD was in her band. I don't remember remarking on it, partly because Rosalyn had, as usual, assembled a big drunken ensemble of friends to back her up and for some reason Craig Bougie wasn't doing sound; they had some new guy doing it. As often happens with that, the acoustic instruments just didn't make it into the mix. It was all *bam bam bam, wheedly wheedly wheedly, bam.* So I'd seen her play but not heard her and that's why I hadn't connected her yet with the kid we'd seen busking by the fence at the Calgary Folk Fest a couple years before.

She approached me. And to this day that is one of my proudest achievements as a musician. The fact that *she* approached *me* and said, "Hey, you're Mykola. I heard your song on the CBC when I was driving the other day. We should play together."

Wow. Even now that kind of takes my breath away. That someone that wonderfully musical felt it was important that we play together. When someone that special wants to play with you, that's better than a Juno. Better than a Grammy.

I didn't know. I was sort of *suspecting* there was something special about this person, so I didn't give her the brush-off, but I was skeptical, because a lot of music is bad. I asked her where she was based, and she said she was living in Victoria, and by chance, I was playing there the next weekend at Tuesday's.

I told her that I couldn't promise anything but if she showed up early for sound check we could maybe try running a couple of tunes.

I have trouble when people want to play with me but they aren't very good. I usually act like I'm drunker than I am and fall over or something to avoid further conversation, so I was taking a big risk by not falling over but instead agreeing to try playing with her. Part of me was hoping she wouldn't show up so I wouldn't have to find some way of ducking out of it if she wasn't good. Although I did have a good feeling about her.

I was both pleasantly and unpleasantly surprised when I arrived from the ferry to Tuesday's and she was already there, drinking a muddy Caesar. That would be the first and only time she was ever early for anything in the whole time I've known her.

I said, "Wow, you're here already," and she said, "I said I would be," acting almost offended, like we'd known each other for years.

I suggested we go in the back-office area and try running something together. I'd been picking over trying to do a version of your song "Iron Grey" in a Ukrainian kind of mode, and so I got out the kobza and she tuned to me, and we went into it.

It was really strange.... It was really strange....

The way her violin blended with the kobza, it was like they were made out of wood from the same tree. I know that sounds cheesy. Sorry. But it's a fact that as the song played through, she and I knew what we were gonna do before we knew we knew it.

As we strolled through the words and the chord changes, the song achieved a new layer of meaning. I had a sudden realization that the song, which I had thought of as just a simple love song, was about hiding as much as it was about loving. It was about a tension between loving and hiding. I hadn't understood the song properly before.

When it was finished, I thought of the thing that the manager of the Grand Ole Opry said to Bill Monroe, who would one day be famous as the inventor of bluegrass music, when Monroe had shown up out of nowhere to audition for the Opry. When Monroe had finished playing his audition piece, the manager said, "Not only are you hired, if you ever leave, you're gonna have to fire yourself."

NAME WITHHELD

BELFAST, 2013

I WAS STILL DRINKING QUITE HEAVILY BACK THEN. I brought DD back to mine, but we soon ran out of booze. I still live in the same place, a little house that belonged to my gran, built about a hundred years ago. Last decorated in the early sixties. I don't mind it that way. It reminds me of her. She saved me, when my parents realized what I am and my father kicked me out of the house and my mother stood by and did nothing. Well, what could she do? What could she ever do? I'd feel sorry for her maybe if it wasn't me, her child, who she failed to protect. But I find I can only afford to feel so many things, and I'm afraid I can't spare her any pity. My gran took me in and then after some time she took sick and I looked after her, and then she died and I was alone in her house in a neighbourhood that's a fair ways from here. A middle-class neighbourhood. A unionist neighbourhood.

I put a can of cider in DD's hand and she brought her fiddle out and started playing a tune she'd learned in the pub in Galway. I told her to hold off because the houses are built very close to each other and the walls are very thin. A neighbour of mine down the street had brought some musicians back after the bar the previous summer and they'd played some tunes, you understand, and later someone had thrown a brick through their front window.

That was how it was still then. The poetry café in the arcade (before it burned down under suspicious circumstances) had a poster on the wall beside the till with a picture of the city with a giant cartoon rainbow over it, and a large caption that said, "Belfast 2002: Still A Bit Shite" in large rainbow letters.

I don't know if you could still get a brick through your window if people heard traditional Irish tunes coming out of your house. Nowadays they probably couldn't be arsed. I suppose that's a good thing.

At any rate, we sat and talked and drained what was left of the booze in the house, which wasn't much as I hadn't done the shopping, and when I realized we were fresh out I also realized that all the shops had closed for the night.

I don't drink anymore but back then I was drinking fairly steadily, and I got the sense that so was DD, so we were in a difficult position. We didn't want to be seen by the men DD had left behind, who were probably still out on the piss somewhere, but we were desperate for a drink and the shops were all closed.

I remember saying, "Do you want to go to a gay bar? I'll bet you thought we didn't have one, but we do."

Of course, I meant the Kremlin, which is utter shite now, but back then wasn't so bad. It's ten times the size it was then, now, and the staff they have now on the door are, God, they're fucking evil. I stopped going when I was out with some people and we left another bar and they turned us away because it was "only enough capacity for regulars." Regulars. Fuck me. I was there on fucking opening night when we all had to dash out in an orderly fashion because of a bomb threat. That fuckwit cunt was still shitting his wee nappies when we were — God, I sound old and I know it. Never mind.

At any rate, we were out of booze, and this was a crisis, and so we went out.

I hadn't been out for a while, and we actually had decent craic. DD thought that was *hilarious*, the word *craic*. "Crack? Really? It's *all* good crack?"

I said, "It just means fun. Fun times."

"Right," she said, "just like in the Downtown Eastside in Vancouver!"

As I was just after telling you, the Kremlin was special then. It was special for Belfast to have a gay bar at all. Before, there had just been a few pubs where it was known that the barman would tolerate benders and dykes, but those bars weren't *for* us. You couldn't kiss and hold hands, which you actually could do in the Kremlin, just like a proper gay bar anywhere. The first song on the first night of the Kremlin was, of course, "I Will Survive," and I remember I did, in fact, have a bit of a cry while it was playing, so I did. I saw other people crying, too, while they were dancing; it was a bit ridiculous, dancing, wiping your eye, dancing, wiping your eye, to this song which is such a cliché of queer life, but still, you know, has this power to it. "As long as I know how to love." My favourite part is the epic string part with no singing in it at all, the swelling strings, like a gay disco symphony — they still get me every time. Although the singer, what's her name, Gloria Gaynor, she's a marvellous singer as well, of course. I wish I could sing like that. I wish I could play any instrument.

By the time I brought DD to the Kremlin people were already saying that it wasn't what it had once been, that it was losing its sense of community like, that all the cocaine in the toilets and the other drugs were ruining it. But looking back, it was still quite something. And it was still quite a risky place to go. No one had the guts to actually go in and bash anybody on the inside of the place, they were probably afraid that if the mirror ball light hit them in just the wrong way it might turn them gay, but you could still easily get jumped on outside by some of these wee bastards who had nothing better to do because they were too ugly to pull a bird or perhaps they were closet benders themselves and couldn't admit it. Sometimes they would jump on us as we came round the corner or sometimes they would just sit on a wall drinking cans of American lager and shout at us as we went in or out. Or there were "family groups" of men who would wait outside the Kremlin to "knock some sense" into their queer cousin, or perhaps they'd decided that someone's older boyfriend had turned them gay and they needed to be warned off in a nasty way. And they would sometimes be watching you as you went in and out and perhaps throw a bottle at you to pass the time, and of course back then the police would do nothing about it. It's a bit better now, but only just. Oh, I even heard about the paramilitary groups on both sides being involved in enforcing straightness, like, back then. You think I'm making it up. Well, I wish I was.

I hate that feeling when you've been drinking, right, and then you stop drinking, and your levels go down. It makes you feel tired and listless and hopeless. There we were at the bar, and the music was going, and people were dancing, and we had our first beer, and it just wasn't working. We didn't feel like dancing. We were just quite tired, and we'd come all the way here on the bus, so we didn't want to waste the trip by yawning our way through DD's first night at a gay bar in Belfast. So this was the first night that I was introduced to Red Bull and vodka, as a drink. It was DD's idea. It tasted like candy, and as soon as it went down you felt this mad chemical energy welling up in you. Then we started to have a proper good time.

I don't dance as much now. I suppose I should. It's good for you to dance, but I don't. That night we really danced. We danced in a completely not–Northern Ireland way: we had no inhibitions, and we were not afraid to be completely silly. We did our best imitations of sixties boogaloo dances like Shoot the Pony and the Mashed Potato. DD grabbed me, which I don't normally like, but for some reason, I don't know, it didn't bother me with her, and we pretended to tango back and forth across the room, although neither of us knew how to tango properly. And if people looked at us cattily and judged us, we didn't feel their looks. What's amazing is that it felt like for once no one was judging, like everyone looking on was enjoying our pure enjoyment of the music as we danced our silly dances.

It's not so clever now, but since it was such early days, it seemed quite funny that they called it "'90s Night: Instant Nostalgia." We danced to all kind of ridiculous songs like "Smells Like Teen Spirit" and Madonna's "Vogue." Yeah, we *vogued*. It was hilarious, with this kind of mysterious under-note of sadness. It was strange to be already nostalgic for something that had only just passed, and hadn't been that good anyway, to be honest. But the nostalgia was real. We were still young then, but something about that night, which was such good craic, also felt like the beginning of saying goodbye to our youth.

It was quite a night. It was one of the best nights out I've ever had, really, and that's probably why I still remember DD after all this time. I remember telling her some things about myself that I'd never told anyone up to that point. Not even my gran. I wrote a poem about that night which I managed to get published in a magazine, some writers' collective that disbanded ten years ago at least. I think I still have a copy of it in the house somewhere. Oh, that's how you found me. Well, I'm pleased that you kept that. Right. It was so long ago.

PETE PODEY

HIS HOME STUDIO, BASEMENT SUITE,
GRAVELY STREET, OFF COMMERCIAL DRIVE,
VANCOUVER, 2015

MYKOLA WAS BOOKED TO BE artist-in-residence at the festival in Belfast. I don't remember the name of it now.

I got there before Mykola but after DD, who had gone early. It was my job to look into making sure our technical requirements were met, because, I wouldn't say he was a space cadet exactly, but Mykola doesn't always have the finest handle on logistics.

Okay, so, I got there and got driven from Belfast airport by a guy named Brian who was ex-IRA but now worked as a driver for the festival. It was a long ride in from the airport, and I wouldn't have known what to say to Brian about his past, because, although he was a super-nice guy, I mostly think of myself as a pacifist, and I try to be nice to people but at the same time, I didn't want to endorse violence. Luckily Brian did pretty much all the talking. I remember thinking, *How did this guy survive for thirty years in a secret military group, being such a super Chatty Cathy?* I always imagined those guys as kinda tight-lipped, close-to-the-vest, you know? But maybe he was talking so much because he'd saved it up for thirty years.

He told a long story about when Martin Sheen, the movie star, came in for the festival. He took Martin Sheen back to his elderly mother's house (Brian's elderly mother, not Martin Sheen's) and

Martin tried a bowl of Brian's mother's Guinness stew and Martin Sheen the movie star agreed that Brian's mother's stew was the best stew he had ever tasted and said that there certainly was no Irish stew in America that could hold a candle to it. That was the entire point of the story. I remember I was fighting to stay awake through the jet lag and also, okay, the story itself (sorry if that sounds mean), thinking, *Geez, before the peace accord this guy might have been blowing up my hotel or something, and now he's just driving this car, boring me to death.* Which was a weird thing to think, and I guess kind of unfair, but it sure was weird overtop of the jet lag — plus we were driving through these neighbourhoods full of giant painted murals of dead masked Catholic and Protestant terrorists with angel's wings on their backs and machine guns in their hands, with captions that said things like, "*Their only crime was loyalty!*"

When I got to the festival headquarters, there was no accommodation for me arranged, because they had asked Richard Wren in an email what time does your artist arrive, and he had just checked with Mykola about when *he* was arriving. So, they didn't know I needed accommodations. In fact, they hadn't even known I was coming that day; Brian had picked me up by mistake when he was supposed to have picked up Desmond Dekker, the Jamaican ska star.

Luckily, DD had already found a place to stay, and a person to stay with. DD has a way of doing that. She'd made a friend in just a couple weeks in Belfast, a good enough friend to stay with. And, like a lot of times, I was grateful that DD *did* have a way of doing that.

You know, like in football, there's a guy who carries the ball and runs with it (I don't know that much about football), but then there's this guy whose job it is not to carry the ball, but to clear the way forward for the guy with the ball, the sort of vanguard guy?

Well, DD was kind of like that for me, socially. Not that I was the guy with the ball, unless you count my own consciousness, if you will, as my personal ball. But that's getting a little too deep for what I was trying to say. What I mean is, DD had this ability to instantly connect with cool people, and my ability is, like I mentioned before, to *not* be seen by people, so our abilities can be kind of complementary. Although it can sometimes seem like I'm dependent on DD to be seen and that's it, but DD has never seen it that way. That's how she is, and I appreciate that.

DD was there at the festival office with her new friend. I think it was 2002? I feel kinda bad about this now, but at the time, I was still in the mode of "is this a guy or a girl? How do I find out?" Now I wouldn't care. Not that I cared then, but I wondered more then than I would now. I mean, I didn't know as much about transgender people or people who nowadays go by "they," but really I have no idea whether DD's friend, whose name escapes me, whether they would be a they now or not. It was a long time ago now.

Anyway, DD's friend took us back to their house and made us tea and toast with beans, and it was just nice. It was like being at your gramma's house. It was better than being in a hotel. It was maybe the most comfortable couch I've ever slept on. It's pretty important to get decent sleeps on the road.

MYKOLA LOYCHUCK

GREEN ROOM AREA, RUDOLSTADT-FESTIVAL, RUDOLSTADT, GERMANY, 2015

IT WAS A BIG DEAL FOR ME OPENING for Jimmy Kinnock for the first time. He was my hero, growing up. It was my biggest break so far, and I really hoped that if I could impress the Wrens, Jimmy's managers, with my new material I would be on the path to Jimmy-like success and I could be a full-time touring act that could pay my band and everything. [Sighs.]

The show went well, I think, although I made some mistakes and missed some chords. At least we sold lots of albums after our set. And I thought Jimmy was fantastic. Played all my favourites, told funny stories, and he did that thing he does where he talks about the place he's playing in a knowing way, referencing local issues and experiences he's had there. He'd been in Belfast the night Margaret Thatcher stepped down, so he talked about the wild party they'd had that night, and he talked about videos of cats swinging off ceiling fans. He was wonderful. I was in a special place.

Watching him play the old hits, though, the ones everybody wanted to hear, I couldn't help wondering, *Isn't he bored, playing that song for the thousandth time, this song he wrote when he was twenty years old? He's a sensitive, intelligent guy. Does he ever feel like a trained monkey up there?* Not that I'd have said anything like that out loud. I mean, who am I to even speak to an idol, a hero like that?

They called him back for the encore, and he sang "What a Wonderful World" — the Sam Cooke song, not the Louis Armstrong one. It has that neat little rhyme with "science book" paired up with "the French I took." A real pretty soul song, and he sang it with warmth, with Welsh soul, like Tom Jones but without the ugly macho bluster. It was lovely. Lovelier than anything he'd done all night. He was so connected to it, like he was singing it for an old flame, a secret lover from his past who was somewhere hidden in the audience. That's how it felt.

DD and I lost each other in the crowd. I guess I just wanted to be by myself to listen to Jimmy. I saw her when I went backstage to pack up before we headed to the after-party. I saw Jimmy in his dressing room. He was drinking a bottle of beer with a towel over his neck, like a boxer, just decompressing. He raised the bottle at me and smiled and I waved, but I could tell he didn't want to be bothered. I went into our dressing room and started puttering around, getting my stuff together — everyone's always amazed at how quickly I can turn a room into a sprawling mess of my scattered crap — and I saw DD just march right into Jimmy's, *the* Jimmy Kinnock's dressing room, next door. I thought maybe she was drunk and had the wrong room. I got up to go grab her but the talking between them had started, so I hung back in my own room, lurking and listening.

"Hey, Jimmy." So casual.

"Hey, DD. How's it going?" He already knew her name. How did she do that?

"Pretty good. We couldn't find a place to eat before the show, though, so we had to eat PowerBars."

"Do you like PowerBars, DD?"

"Yeah, they're okay, but they give me the shits sometimes."

Welsh laughter.

"Hey, I just wanted to say great show tonight. I really loved the encore, where you stopped being 'Jimmy Kinnock' and just played music, you know? You really sang."

This pretty much blew my mind. She was waltzing into the most famous folksinger in the world's dressing room and actually insulting his set right to his face. And his reaction blew my mind even more.

He gave a long exhale and then he said, "Yeah, I get pretty tired of being 'Jimmy Kinnock' sometimes. Jimmy's not even my real first name. It's my middle name. My real first name's Brian. Thanks for noticing. That means a lot coming from you. I love your playing." I almost died hearing that. It was too much for me.

CARLA PATTERSON

HER STRIP BAR, PORT ——, 2015

HER MOM WAS REALLY FUCKEN WEIRD. She could be super awful crazy, and she could be supercool, too. The uncool shit was kind of infinite. I mean, she adopted DD because she figured if she got a hold of a baby her husband would quit drinking out of a sense of responsibility. No, yah. Men do that all the time, right? [Laughs uproariously.] She picked her out of a bunch of Indian babies up for adoption 'cause DD looked the whitest, although her birth dad was Sioux, I think. So, although old Rotraut liked me, personally, she didn't really like the idea of DD hanging around with me, because I was brown, and I think she had this feeling like she was doing DD a favour by keeping the brown out of her, you know. Letting her be part of *whiteness*. And she wasn't just super-culty Christian, she was *German* super-culty Christian. Yeah. Think about that.

No, I'm not prejudiced against Germans. Fuck you. Oh, you're joking. Okay I get it. No, really, her mom would sit you down at the table at dinner and explain that Hitler wasn't completely all bad, he got the country back to working and he built those awesome autobahns and he loved nature and protected the forests and stuff. And after all, the Jews did control the banks, and killing them all wasn't the right way to go about dealing with it, but it was *still* a problem, you know? And she'd be explaining this to you over the kartoffels (that's what she called her version of potatoes, which were awesome) while DD's dad was sucking on a Lucky, holding a .22 and sighting it out the open window at the woodshed, where the rats were. And she'd be like, "Hitler wasn't so bad as he was painted, you know," and there'd be a "b-chow!" from the ricochet off the woodshed. Quite the meals.

Yeah, when DD told her she was gay, that didn't go over too well. That was what led to the final breakaway, for sure. And having to get the Ministry involved and shit. I almost forgot about all that.

But there was the cool parts. *My* white parents didn't drive me to swimming, *my* parents didn't drive me to fucken Nanaimo for violin lessons. They didn't cook for me the way her mom did. DD was always fed. Good German cooking. I still go over to her mom's for kartoffels now sometimes, even though she's crazy as a shithouse rat. There was some years when I didn't, but I do now again. And she taught DD *skills*, which I wish I had. They were mostly skills for being the good Jehovah's wife, but still, it's good to know how to sew clothes, and keep chickens, and cook kartoffels.

And with motor vehicles, DD's mom was cool. She said she wanted to be a race-car driver but her husband wouldn't let her. What does that mean? There's a lot in there. She had this ambition, and this drunk chain-smoking asshole put his foot down and said no. It's fucked up, because he wasn't a Jehovah guy, or if he was, he wasn't a good one. But because she *was* a good one, she had to obey her husband, even if he was less, you know, holy than she was. Fucked up, eh?

But man she was a demon behind the wheel. That woman could make any car or truck rock 'n' roll. And on the back roads? It was *insane*. She had this Oldsmobile Cutlass Supreme, from about 1982, big fucker of a car, and I think she'd done some mods to the engine? Bored it out and put in some Weber carbs or something? Or maybe she dropped some fucken giant truck engine into it or something? And the suspension was all tight. There was extra bars and shit. She did all her own mechanical work. She would just rip out on that thing. We loved it. Even when we were like twelve. It was like an amusement-park ride. We'd be out on some bumpy gravel logging road, and she'd say, "Do you wanna go *faster*?!" and we'd be like, "*Yeah*!!" and she'd say, "Keep your tongues inside your teeth!" and she would jam the pedal down, do some real quick gear shifting and we'd just shoot down those roads, sliding through the turns, almost hit a tree sometimes. She was fucking invincible in the driver's seat.

Her sister was the same. Auntie Ina. Auntie Ina would be like, "Now, what do we do when we see a p'leece car, girls?" and we were trained to say, "Gun it, breathe, then gear up, gear up, gear up!" Yeah. It was like the normal rules they followed when it came to women being all meek and obedient somehow didn't apply to driving. I'm not sure why.

And her mom taught her a ton of shit about engines and all. They took this old '70s Kawasaki motorcycle that had been sitting in the barn forever, and they totally tore the motor down and rebuilt it. And she just gave it to DD. DD didn't even have a licence. She'd drive it all over the back roads. I'd ride bitch with her. Till one time we were going hard on the Golden Wedding and she looked down and saw the gas gauge was close to empty. She said, "Whisky makes me go. It'll make my bike go, too!" … which sounded like it made sense at the time but it totally ruined the bike. Strangely, her mom didn't freak out about that. She was just like, "Well, that's what you get." Which was not how she reacted when DD told her she was gay. Nope.

PETE PODEY

HIS HOME STUDIO, BASEMENT SUITE, GRAVELY STREET, OFF COMMERCIAL DRIVE, VANCOUVER, 2015

BELFAST TURNED OUT TO BE A KIND OF exciting place to be, and the festival was especially exciting. Because the peace accords had only happened a couple years before, and it seemed like people were slowly dropping the importance of whether they were Catholic or Protestant and realizing that it also mattered what kind of city Belfast was going to be in the future. Was it going to be a cool bohemian European city like Berlin or Barcelona, or was it going to be a nasty, materialist, car-filled shithole like Calgary or Dallas or Stuttgart? That was the new struggle going on. You could see that both the Barcelonians and the Calgarians wanted peace equally, but the Barcelonians wanted peace so they could have the Royal Dutch Ballet come and perform or have poetry slams and stuff, and the Calgarians wanted peace so they could have Orange Mobile phone stores and all-night 7-Elevens and IKEA. That was the new struggle, and we had landed in the middle of a festival run by people who were definitely on the Barcelona side of things.

When Mykola arrived they moved us to the house of this lady who worked for the festival. She was Scottish but she'd married an Irish musician and then divorced him but stayed in Belfast. She liked to party and other artists and musicians would wind up back there at the end of the night and Mykola and DD would swap songs and tell loud funny stories with them till what DD called "fuck o'clock."

We'd wake up fuzzy every day about ten in the morning, with the hostess where we were staying telling us Sean from the festival was on the phone. We were the first artists-in-residence he'd ever had so he was always asking us *if* we wanted to do something. "Do you want to play in between sets at a photo exhibit launch? Do you want to be videotaped playing Ukrainian folk songs in a taxi cab driving through a poor Unionist neighbourhood for Irish national television? Do you want to play to a dozen cultural attachés on a boat in the middle of the river at noon?" And Mykola always said yes even though some of the times we could have really used another couple hours of sleep.

At first DD's friend would come along for the ride on these things. But you could tell they were a little weirded out by it all. Shy, I guess. I mean, I'm shy, but I would just hang in the background and play the drum. I would disappear, but DD's friend seemed kind of … uncomfortable.

Like when we were out on the River Liffey? Was it? No, the Lagan. That's right, playing to all those cultural people, they had strawberries, cream, and champagne for everybody. I took some, although I was careful not to take too much, and Mykola was really wolfing it down because he'd taken a half-hour shower and missed breakfast. DD's friend wouldn't take any, as if they felt they had no right or something. I don't think Mykola noticed that at all, but he was pretty wound up.

The thing with Patti Smith was the last time I saw DD's friend. I think it was the last straw maybe. It was kinda funny, actually, the attitude toward Patti Smith in Belfast.

Sean didn't call up on the phone for that one, he actually came by the house. We were hauling ourselves out of our sleeping bags on the floor, and Mykola was trying to make coffee but just basically annihilating the kitchen without really producing any coffee. I had to turn the wrong burner off on the stove and turn the right one on, twice, which I did quietly without him noticing, so he could actually get the kettle going. I don't mean to disparage Mykola, 'cause he's a great guy and an amazing songwriter, but really I don't know how he travels throughout the world without burning down every house he stays at.

Anyway, Sean was there at the table with a mug of tea, and we were all sitting round the table but he was really only talking to Mykola.

He'd said, "Here's the thing, Myko. Patti Smith is playing tonight."

"Wow! She's one of my big heroes."

Sean said, "Yeah! Yeah, me too. We're extremely pleased to have her. I am. I dreamed that one day we might be able to get her, and this year, we did. It's amazing."

"So, what's this about? We're not opening for her, too?"

"Ah, no. Her twenty-five-year-old guitar-player boyfriend is playing support. That's in her contract."

"She gets a twenty-five-year-old guitar-player boyfriend in her contract?"

"No. He's her boyfriend. And she insists that he play before her."

"Okay. I understand that. So, what's up?"

"Well, Myko, it's like this … er … it's like, I was really lookin' forward to having Patti Smith at the festival, like, but now … well … now I can't really face talking to her. She's too huge a figure in my personal world. I can't even hardly speak to her. And it's normally my job to introduce the headliners but … well … I can't. So … I was wondering if you would do it."

That's when DD piped up. "Are you sure she wants an introduction?"

And Mykola, who also didn't want to confront Patti Smith face to face, picked up on that. I knew he didn't like to be onstage when he didn't have an instrument in his hands. He was, I guess, kinda eager to deke out of it, so he said, "Yeah. Maybe you should ask her if she even *wants* an introduction."

And then Sean brightened up and said, "Well, perhaps *you* could go backstage and ask her if she wants an introduction?"

It was like watching a game of hot potato. Nobody wanted to actually talk to Patti Smith. But since it was Mykola suggesting that she didn't want an introduction, he could see it fell to him to ask.

When we went backstage, there was Patti Smith in the same room that Jimmy Kinnock had been in. I did my thing of being kind of there but not there, hanging back, making myself invisible. I wanted to see what all this was going to be like.

She was smoking. There was a sign up saying NO SMOKING. But she was smoking and nobody was going to tell Patti Smith to put out her smoke, that's for sure. I remember she had a very pronounced moustache. Her cute twenty-five-year-old guitar-player boyfriend was tuning up this shiny goldtop Gibson Les Paul in the corner.

Sean barely managed to stutter out the introductions. He called her "Ms. Smith." He didn't look directly at her when he shook her hand, although she attempted to make eye contact.

It was the same with Mykola. He was super mumbly, studying the scuffed toes on his combat boots. She kept trying to get him to meet her gaze, but he just couldn't do it. Naturally, she didn't even notice I was there. We had all asked DD to come, but she said she had some Guinness-drinking to do, so she wasn't there and neither was her friend.

To everybody's relief, Ms. Smith said she didn't want an introduction. She said she'd rather just go onstage and start. Audible sighs of relief. Audible.

I can't really describe it, but it was an amazing show. And being the official people who were, uh, not introducing her, we got to watch the whole show from the wings, invisible to the audience, twenty feet away from her.

It was so cool to watch how the whole show worked. There was a lot of dry ice for atmosphere, and she had something kinda flowy on, like she was a kind of Priestess of Rock, and she closed her eyes a lot, like she was going into some other world or something. Okay but I noticed something really neat about the set she did with her band — it was being made up on the fly, but in a supertight way.

I mean, if you watched the drummer and the bass player, and you watched what they were watching, you started to see that they were watching her hands really close. And then you watched those fluttering, expressive hands, and you realized you were watching a really intense kind of sign language, a set of signals.

And when we were hanging out later, I had a little chat with the drummer (who I noticed was like me and sort of made a point of not being noticed), and it turned out I wasn't wrong: there was this complex bunch of gestures she would do, like a baseball catcher does to tell the pitcher what kind of pitch to throw. If she wanted to extend the solo, she'd do one thing, and if she wanted to bring the volume down so she could really whisper her vocal, she did another. She was totally running the whole band with these little signals the whole time. I told DD about it, but she didn't seem that impressed. I was like, "Isn't that amazing? She's actually orchestrating the performance with her hands!" and DD was like, "That's why I got out of classical music. I play with you guys to feel something. Not to be some kind of trained seal." That really surprised me, but then later I realized she was right. We were good because we never knew what we were gonna do until we did it, and when it went especially well, the audience could feel that we were just as surprised as they were. I mean, I already knew that, but she reminded me of it. She's good that way.

Then we were at the after-after-after-party at some lock-in session at some pub. DD was sitting with her friend, and DD was wearing her friend's hat, which was this kind of beat-up wide-brimmed fedora, and who should come in but Smith herself. I don't know if she was drunk or what, but she spotted DD and just made a beeline for her.

I could see DD's friend registering this fact, that Patti Smith was heading right at them, there seemed to be something about Patti Smith that just scared the shit out of DD's pal, like it did everyone else in Belfast. Patti Smith came up to DD, pointed at the hat, and shouted, "Hey! I had a hat just like that!"

And DD looked up, didn't even do a double take. She just looked up from her beer and said, "The fuck you did."

And the whole pub kind of gasped.

And Patti Smith said, "Did you steal my hat?" but she was smiling. She was *enjoying* this little sparring match.

And DD said, "This is my fuckin' hat, bitch!"

And Smith was still unfazed and unoffended. She said, "Well, can I try it on for a second?"

And DD looked at her mock-suspiciously, narrowed her eyes, and said, "Well, I dunno. Can I trust you to give it back? How do I know you won't just fuck off with it?"

And Smith went, "Trust me."

DD started to offer the hat, and Smith reached for it, and at the last minute DD whipped it away from Patti Smith and went, "Too slow! Psych! My hat."

And Smith just laughed. She turned to somebody with her and said, "Ha! Bitch stole my hat. Let's get a drink." She walked onto the bar, sticking her tongue out at DD.

And I think that really freaked out DD's friend. It was just too much. Lipping off Patti Smith. We didn't see DD's friend again. Belfast loved Patti Smith so much that Belfast was frightened of Patti Smith. But not DD.

GIULIETTA CAETANO

HER HOUSE, TUCSON, ARIZONA, 2016

JACOB HAD A CONVICTION. So he couldn't legally cross the U.S. border. I don't know for sure what it was for. He's like, what you call an unreliable witness. I know he wasn't lying about having a conviction, but I think he said it was for marijuana possession in Ottawa, but with that one, who the hell knows? Anyway, he couldn't cross the border. So we hit on this idea that he and Tom would just walk across the border from Alberta into Montana, and we would drive across and pick them up on the other side.

We looked at the Milk River on the map, and it looked like if you just followed it, you'd eventually wind up in America. It's a big long border. They couldn't be guarding every inch of it. Mexicans crossed over the southern border all the time. They couldn't possibly be watching the Canadian border even half as much. Right?

The reason it seemed like a reasonable plan was that we were all out of our little minds. And the reason for *that* was the Calgary Stampede at the height of the oil boom.

Stampede is just nuts, man. And not in a good way. It's hard-working, pig-ignorant, bad people who believe they're good people, and they have too much money and they're cutting loose and they think they really deserve to party because they've been working so hard fucking up the Earth the rest of the year.

At the centre of it is a rodeo that kills about twenty perfectly healthy, beautiful horses a year. I never saw any of the barrel races or bucking broncs. We didn't see any of the events. Where were we? We were at the epicentre of the party. Ground zero: a bar called Steerpunchers [ed: bar name has been changed for legal reasons].

We had heard there was good busking money to be made at the Stampede, in particular if you played country music. We played country music. Well, we played country songs. We just played them after snorting a bunch of speed. It accidentally started sounding like bluegrass.

We were totally unprepared for what Stampede was. It's when regular people in Calgary try to be like we were all the time. They book ten days off work, leave the office, sit down at the first available bar stool, and just *go* till they can't go no more. Stampede's in July and I bet there's a whole bunch of mysterious-looking children in Alberta that have birthdays in what? ... August, September ... in April. Come to think of it, there're a lot more women named April in Alberta than anywhere else I've been anywhere.

Bars open all night. Drunk pancake breakfasts in the morning with the local politicians plastered to the gills and handing out beers at 9:00 a.m. Public make-out sessions between Stetson-hatted men and women with hair as high as the hats, the making-out crossing the line into full-on public genital groping and more. Fist fights in the streets, and the cops just looking on and laughing. It's *crazy,* man. Especially in a place that's ultra-judgmental about people who drink or do drugs the rest of the year.

We got set up downtown and started into our set, and, my God almighty, the money rained down. I've never seen anything like it before or since. I guess oil was worth a lot of money and everybody was making a ton and it was just spilling everywhere. Later we saw ads in the paper in Winnipeg trying to get dishwashers for the

Denny's in downtown Calgary, advertising twenty bucks an hour. You couldn't get a shuttle ride from the airport because nobody wanted to work for the chickenshit wages of a shuttle driver. There was just so much money sloshing around. All you had to do was play some country music with big energy and put your hat out and catch it as it fell. That's what we did. Man, I sure would be happy to have that kind of cash money right now, I'll tell you that much.

We did this for a couple days. We got ourselves a couple rooms at a Motel 6 on the outskirts of town and we just rolled around in the money. And the cocaine! It was a blizzard, man. People would throw little eight balls in the hat. No shit. Jacob would scoop those up right away in mid-verse.

I swear, we made so much money. Definitely the most I ever made playing music. Where did it all go? We would have so much change that we'd keep it in these metal tool boxes. One time, me and Jacob took these tool boxes into the Royal Bank of Canada branch downtown, and we come up to the wicket — maybe, okay, looking a little rough, hadn't bathed in a while, tattoos, raggedy denim — and we clank these tool boxes full of change on the shelf of the teller's window, and smile in what I thought was a friendly way, and then I realize she's actually reaching down to push the robbery panic button. It was like, "Hey, lady! Hello? Just looking to get some bills here." God, Calgary could be a super-straight town. Except when it wasn't.

Right about then was when things took a turn for the crazier.

We were busking on the street corner downtown around four or five in the afternoon, had a good little after-work crowd for our World Land-Speed Record version of "Flowers on the Wall," and this big tall guy in white jeans and a white leather cowboy jacket with white leather fringe came up. White cowboy hat, too. That goes without sayin'. This dude was a vision. We finished the song and he said, "You guys ever do corporate events?" and we were like, "Whuh?"

He threw his business card down in Tom's mandolin case and said, "We're putting on a champagne luncheon tomorrow for our best customers. Come down to the address on the card at 1:00 p.m., it's a thousand bucks for a half-hour set. You guys know any Johnny Cash songs?"

"Um, yeah."

"Okay, then. See you about noon? Address is on the card. You guys'll be a great addition to the party. Free sandwiches and champagne!" He walked away. The card was from some giant specialized tool-making company.

The event was truly weird. Normal people in these outfits that were a dumb combination of normal clothes and cowboy costumes, most of them our parents' age, capering around, jumping on desks, spinning the chairs, grabbing each others' asses, shouting.... A lot of random shouting and whooping. A number of the men were these barrel-chested, muscular fat guys. They were mostly wearing blue jeans and brand-new white cowboy shirts with bolo ties and, of course, cowboy hats, like most of the men and women at Stampede. Their proportions and the way they were acting made them seem like giant three-year-olds at some rich toddler's birthday party. But there were no parents, no grown-ups around to supervise.

For the most part, nobody was paying any attention to us. They were all so drunk. But then the guy in white brought his buddy over. Kind of a nondescript, middle-aged white dude. We were in the middle of a song when he stood in front of us, right in Jacob's face.

"Do you know who this is?"

Jacob just hung on a chord, chucking away, vamping. He kind of brought the conversation into the song, like a talking blues.

"Do I know who *who* is?"

"Do you know who *this* is?

"No, I don't know who *this* is. Who (chucka chucka chucka) is (chucka chucka chucka) this? (chucka chucka chucka)"

"This is the owner of Steerpunchers."

"Hey, that's great! I've heard of that. I hear that it's a great big cowboy bar."

"It's the best goddamn bar in the world."

"Cool."

"This guy wants to hire you."

"Hire me?"

"Hire all of you."

"To play? (chucka chucka chucka)"

"To play on the Steerpunchers bus."

"To play on the Steerpunchers bus?"

"To play for the people on the Steerpunchers bus."

"Is that a special (chucka chucka chucka) short bus (chucka chucka chucka) for cowboys? (chucka chucka chucka)"

"It's the bus that takes everybody from the Stampede grounds to Steerpunchers. It's a party bus."

And it sure was. Holy Jesus.

Look, I'm getting to the story of how we wound up trying to run the border, but I'm first trying to give you an insight into our state of mind when we made the plan. The Steerpunchers bus is the key to understanding where we were at.

Steerpunchers was the most popular bar in Calgary. It was kind of a party institution among normal people in Alberta. It was like they saw that movie *Urban Cowboy* and they decided to make a bar that replicated every cliché of the city cowboy bar. Man, it was huge, too.

Hell, yes, there were mechanical bulls. And taxidermy on the walls. And Miller Lite neon signs, and all that. The waitresses and barmaids all wore high heels and short skirts and tight T-shirts that a lot of them had tied up around their tits, Daisy Duke–style. There were tits everywhere. It was a cavalcade of tits. The bar could have been named Tits and Cocaine for Fake Cowboys and that would have been, like, truth in advertising.

The waitresses had holsters on their hips with tequila bottles in them, and bandoliers of shot glasses, and you could do shots off their tits. Even girls who were just customers would let guys do shots off their tits. It was known that if a waitress wanted to have a boob job, the bar owner would pay for it. There were a lot of hyper-inflated boobs bouncing around.

And then there were these pools scattered around the bar. Bouncy inflatable pools. And it was understood that any random cowboy could pick up any random cowgirl in the bar and just laughingly drop them in one of these pools. And the girls responded by giggling and looking down at their tits and saying something like "Oh, my goodness! My T-shirt is all wet! Tee-hee!" It was insane. It was scary. The pools were full of ice water, to make the nipples stand up. No! You think I'm making this up but I'm totally serious. This is how it was.

Why did the girls let them do it? Girls are raised to let guys get away with all kinds of assholery, or hadn't you noticed, man? And because they were all absolutely shit-faced and coked into monsterland. What was the most common method of doing the coke? You guessed it. Off the tits. Tits, tits, tits.

And when you pour that much tequila into a person, they normally would, you know, fall down, but the cocaine kept people upright like a fast-moving horny zombie. A lot of people were there-not-there. I saw a lot of girls go off with men who I really don't think were their types, just because they were really there-not-there. It was a date-rape extravaganza. People talk a lot about "roofies" and I'm sure that some guys were slipping drugs into girls' drinks, but for the most part, the "roofie" was ten shots of Jose Cuervo. I'll let Tom tell you all about that. No, never mind, forget I said anything. Tom. What a guy. What a shit-show.

And once people were in that state of drunken stimulation, the festival of wealth would happen. Guys waving wads of cash to get the bartender's attention, tipping a fifty. Tipping a hundred. Women screaming out the price of their handbags over the sound of the New Country. "Do you like this? It's Dolce & Gabbana. It's not off the rack. It's from the Rodeo Drive store. It cost my boyfriend five thousand dollars. He's not here tonight. He's in Dallas."

Our job was to help deliver people to this ninth circle of fake ranch-culture debauchery.

The bus was a swanky, two-storey bus that went back and forth between the Stampede grounds and Steerpunchers all night, through to closing time. Our job was to play for people as they rode to the bar. Essentially, our job was to keep the party going. We were pretty good at that. Yes, sir.

We had a solid repertoire of classic country covers that even these poky dummies were familiar with. We played 'em fast and loose, with a lot of call and response. It got people hooked into our deal. They didn't need too much encouragement to sing along. They were already beyond half-cut when they got on the bus. There was plenty of puking. They had to have a full-time cleaner, just for the bus. Lots of sawdust for the puke. One time, I watched a blonde in a nice tight pink dress that looked almost like a swimsuit just laugh as she pissed herself, standing in the aisle between the seats.

They weren't paying a whole lot of close attention to the musical subtleties, if you know what I mean, but we gave them the vibe that the party was still on, that they weren't waiting to get somewhere, they were partying on the bus. And everybody loves Johnny Cash, man. We could have played "Folsom Prison Blues," exclusively, on a constant loop, and nobody would have minded. Most wouldn't have noticed the song hadn't changed. "I hear that train a comin' / comin' round the bend." Also we played "Sixteen Tons," and Tom would fuck around with the lyrics just to entertain us. "I got two fists of iron and the others of steel / if the right ones don't get you then the left ones will." After a few days of it, when it got late, everyone was so messed up that Jacob would do his country version of "Too Drunk to Fuck" and they didn't care. Who's that by? Dead Kennedys, right. I used to think Jacob wrote it. He liked to play it every time some shit-heel made a request for "Friends in Low Places" by Garth Brooks.

We'd deliver the meat to the bar, and then we'd ride back to the Stampede grounds for another load of fucked-up straight people.

Then when the last ride finished, we were invited into the bar itself, to drink for free and party with the staff and owners and preferred customers. That's when the shit got really wild. We used to say it became Steerpuncher-zillas.

As you walked through the parking lot, you could see people fucking in the cabs of trucks, flashes of more tits, asses in the air framed by strings of neon-pink butt-floss thongs, or — Oh! Some nasty hairy man-asses. Plus more puking men and women of all ages and all kinds of fancy dress.

And then you'd walk through the door and it would all hit you at once. The New Country music with its auto-tuned, doubled vocals, standard-issue slamming-car-door eighties snare sound, and perfect fiddle accents would just batter down the doors of your ears. The lights flashed and swivelled around. The giant TVs showing mostly football or boxing — men hitting men, over and over — and you'd think, *Is the free premium tequila and bar manager's personal uncut cocaine stash worth dealing with this?* And we would just think, *Yes. Yes it is.* Because we'd been drinking beer for six hours by then. And just because.

Here's an aspect of it I never figured out: the line dances. Men and women would be just hammered to all hell and gone, like, barely standing, having said the same four phrases in a loop for the last hour, and suddenly a certain Shania Twain song or something would come on, and a switch would click in their tiny little brains, and they'd jump on the dance floor and do the most complicated series of steps and slides and turns and claps and hip throws, all in a line, all in perfect unison, while Shania promised she was "gonna getcha while I gotcha inside." Where did they all learn this shit? I mean, everybody there gave the impression that they'd rather die than learn anything new about anything. Learning dances takes, you know, thinkin' work. And how come they could just jump in there and do it all perfect, like cowgirl robots, after taking all that booze on board? I could never work that out.

You know what? The whole thing scared the living shit out of me. I used to hold my guitar case supertight over my chest, trying to ward off the glowering horny man-stares. I felt like I might need to swing it hard to defend myself at any moment. I don't know why I went along with it all. Probably 'cause DD never seemed afraid. She seemed able to just dive right into it, roll with it all. In her way. You know, she just has this way of kind of fitting right into whatever group she's running with. She's totally matching these hulking bruiser belt-buckle heroes shot for shot. Did she do shots off the waitresses' tits? Hell, yes. You better believe it. DD loved titties. Lines of coke, too. I admit it now, I felt weird about that. We never discussed what our thing was, but I was in love with her. I really was. So, I was drinking to handle the fear, maybe some jealousy, and just because once you start rolling, you're rolling, you know? Damn, I still feel that twinge of jealousy right now sitting here, thinking of her snarfling off those giggling cowgirl cheerleader tits. I still feel that gut twinge of jealousy a little bit, after all the work I've done to try to get myself out of that bad place I was living in back then.

Listen, if you do find DD, could you tell her again that I'm sorry about what happened at the end of our thing? I've really done a lot of work on myself to be a better person than I was. It was a crazy time. Just tell her I'm sorry. No excuses.

TOM ABBOTT

KINGSTON'S SECOND OLDEST BAR, AFTER CLOSING, 2015

I HOST THE OPEN MIC NIGHT HERE. I've been doing it for the last eight fuckin' years now, since I moved out here from Victoria. That's probably too long, but hey, I like it, I get paid enough to cover my rent, and I drink for free which is a good thing and also a problem, sure. But I'm living in the service of the song. That's a sacred duty for me. That's always been a sacred thing to me, even when I was using it for fucked-up shit.

A lot of the songs people play at open mics are bullshit. Either bullshit from the radio, or bullshit they made up out of snatches of words from bullshit songs off the radio, or songs that used to be good but got played way too much. But I play good ones to start the night, and every now and then somebody comes along with the real shit, a real killer song out of nowhere and I try to encourage that with a free beer. Maybe that'll get them further into doing it. Who knows, maybe they'll be the next Joni Mitchell for the fuck I know. I learned how to do this from watching Rosalyn Knight host the Hullaballoo at Tuesday's Bar. She's still the master, fuckin' right. There's just a few rules: treat everybody with respect, whether they're the shaky kid who shows promise or the old rock warrior comin' up to sing "Wish You Were Here." Get their names right —

I mean get the pronunciation right, even if it's some weird name like Rakouthi or something. Don't let people run over their time, but don't be a fuckin' dick about cutting them off when they run over. Kind of clear your throat, or, if that doesn't work, wait till the end of the song and then thank them really loud and ask for a big hand from the audience, who always obliges because they get that the louder they applaud, the easier it'll usually be to get this joker off the stage.

I try to encourage everybody to keep the music happening in their lives, even if they suck. That's my duty here. I believe in it. You could say I'm working in the basement, in the fuckin' dirty old boiler room of the Tower of Song. But a tower is the wrong way to think about songs. DD understands that. We all understood that, in that band. Even Jacob. Maybe especially him. That's what made us fucking great. I still think we were great.

Those days with the Supersonic Grifters. Fuck me, it was wild. I would never go back to that way of living but it was a blast while we were doing it, although it fuckin' sucked ass sometimes. Music was almost always good, though. I didn't realize then how rare that is.

Definitely the attempt to cross the border into Montana was one of the low points. Giulietta blames Steerpunchers? Yeah, maybe. But who decided to get sucked into there? We did. We all got into music for the same reason, that was why we were in a band together, because the music had saved us, at one time or another in our lives. Saved our lives. And then we *used* music to get money, to get drugs, to get fucked. The music had magical powers and we had a through-line to the real shit, and we used that through-line for evil, not for good. Because Steerpunchers, let's face it, was an evil fucking place. It was the evil party at the centre of the evil enterprise of people fucking up the world with evil dirty tar-sands oil.

That's the thing about Calgary, right? The talk is all ranching and the walk is all oil. And oil is fucking evil, obviously. But the West Coast deal is fucking evil, too. It's just not so easy to spot the evil right off the bat. And Kingston. Well. Kingston's got some definite lurking evil, with the prison and all. But in Calgary the evil comes straight atchya.

I was the one who was singing "We gotta get outta this place." I could feel the evil building up in all of us, me included. Oh yeah. And literally, I started to bust into the Animals' song "We Gotta Get Out of This Place" more and more often, playing it in our style, ultra-fast rough country old-timey. 'Cause we never had a setlist, we just finished a song and somebody would start another one, depending on how we felt at the moment. We were that good, that tight, by then, where we all knew what we were gonna play pretty much from the way you counted in the tune. Yeah, that good. And we were using our powers for evil. That's when I got the ptomaine, or the botulism, or whatever it was. Fuuuck.

... What'd Giulietta say about me? What? Hey, because if she was talking shit about me, she wasn't even there for that part. She told you I should tell you about it? Yeah, well, fuckin' right. I'm not proud of it or anything, but I make a point of never being scared of the truth. No, yeah, I'll tell you what happened. It definitely gives you an idea of just how fucked up things were there.

All right, what it was, I was hanging with the evil man, the man in white who was not the owner but was some oil exec or something who got us the gig in the first place. I swear he was the Devil himself. Remember that, kids — the Devil wears white.

Like usual, our band had stumbled into the big ugly bar behind the last of the load of patrons from the Stampede. We were drinking Old Style Pilsner, the beer with the tiny bunnies on it. We were carrying our instruments. Those were our magic talismans that set us apart from the customers and the bar staff and the owners. We were artists. The instruments meant that we weren't living in hell, we were just visiting. As long as we held on to our instruments we were safe. Was the feeling.

It was just another night like the other nights. The usual mayhem was fuckin' roiling. Men in blue Levi's and four-hundred-dollar silk shirts were fanning cash out on the bar to demonstrate their credentials as total assholes, women under heavy eyeshadow were laughing and scanning the room for threats and dreamboats to happiness until they got thrown into the pool to wet them. Toby Keith was blaring, "We'll stick a boot in your ass / it's the American Way," and our band went in different directions. DD and G went to the little girls' room to literally powder their noses, and me and Jacob bellied up to the bar and ordered eighteen-year-old Scotch, which we were given, without a second thought. We had a tradition of knocking back Lagavulin as a double shot first thing. It was the total fuckin' waste of good sipping whisky that was the appeal to us at the time. Then we ordered our thirteenth beers of the night.

Jacob grabbed his by the neck and pulled hard on it. It was fuckin' hot in the place. "This music is killing me. I gotta go kill something back," he said. He strode toward his favourite thing in the place, the *Buck Hunter* video game where you could blow away pixelated deer with a plastic rifle. The way Jacob played the game made me kinda nervous, actually, so I sat alone at the bar and looked at my beer as the warm Scotch feeling came into play in my bloodstream.

Then this fuckin' guy in white, what we in B.C. used to call the Full Nanaimo — hat, shoes, belt, everything — the guy who'd got us the gig, he swung his head out the door of the kitchen and scanned the room. He spotted me. I was one of his favourites, ever since I showed how I can do the whole thing of "I've Been Everywhere" by Hank Snow — I could list all the thousand rhyming place names at about Mach 3 from Boston to Cedar City.

"Hey! Jim! Get in here! I need a hand with this!"

You know, I wish I had more blackouts. A lot of people have blackouts. Women more than men because of, I don't know, something to do with biology, I guess. But it would be great sometimes with some of the stupid fuckin' shit I've done not to remember so much of it. Instead I just get a few tiny blips of non-memory, and mostly more of a blurry thing, like if a drunk guy rolled up against a superrealist painting when the paint was still wet. Sometimes it would be okay with me to just wake up and rub my head and go, "wha' happen?" and have no fuckin' idea how I got somewhere. But I just don't get blackouts, so I remember most of what I've done.

He waved me in, super forceful-like. Bottle of Jose Cuervo Gold in his hand. I don't know why I walked in there — I knew it was a bad idea if it was his idea, but it was sort of like I was hypnotized. He had that kind of power over you. I guess that's leadership, like in the books you see in the airport magazine stores, right?

It was a big high-end professional restaurant kitchen, with all the steel and copper and gas burners you could want. It was closed, there was nobody working, but there was people in there. You bet there was.

There was a chick on the metal food table. She was lying on her back, with her blouse all open and a miniskirt pushed up, and panties down. She was fingering herself, and her mouth was all open. There was another girl bent over the fry grill in nothing but some frilly black underwear; I couldn't see her face. And there was a girl hanging off White Guy with a fancy cowgirl dress half on, half off, rubbing herself on him, licking his neck.

As a former line cook, I noticed somebody had left several burners of the stove on. The blue flame was high as it goes. All the thousands of British thermal units were in play. Next to that, on a counter, a bunch of steaks were thawing. Well, yeah, they'd been left lying around and they were dripping. The word *thawing* in a kitchen is supposed to mean somebody is intending to do something, so I don't know.

The guy shouted, "It's an embarrassment of riches!" waving around the room. He passed me the tequila. Then he spun the half-dressed lady around once and pushed her down on her knees.

She got to work on his belt buckle, and he was like, "Gimme a hand, Jim! Keep one or two of them busy, I can't handle six of 'em!"

So then it gets blurry. I remember kinda making out with the girl with the open blouse, and then seeing the Man in White bent over and making that familiar snuffing sound. At first I thought he was trying to snort raw, melting steak, which somehow made sense to me as something that happened in Calgary. But then I could see there was a healthy-sized pile of blow there. I think I wandered over to get some of that.

Then I remember looking up and I have an image of the guy flipping a steak up in the air with a plastic pancake spatula, his limp dick hanging out of his open pants. I kid you not. The girl in the cowgirl outfit was beside him working it in her hand but not much was happening.

"Huh! It's National Steak-and-Blowjob Day, baby!"

Now, if I'd been in my right mind I would have known that was not a good idea. Everybody knows you only flip steak once or you wind up with steak that looks done but is actually cold and raw on the inside. I knew that. I knew that then.

The girl in her underwear was now doing some blow beside me. Our eyes met and she told me I was good-looking in this slurred voice.

But I was suddenly realizing I was super hungry from the smell of the meat.

So when Mister White shouted, "... and order up!" and flopped a couple steaks back on the counter, I was ready to try it. Which was a total fuckin' mis-steak. Sorry about that. But it really, really was.

I don't remember even looking at it very hard as I scarfed it down, but it was probably some kind of sickly purple-blue on the inside, 'cause I remember the guy looking at me and winking and saying, "Cut off the horns, wipe its ass, and throw it on a plate, hey, pard?" which struck me at the time as a pretty colourful turn of phrase, me coming from Vancouver Island, but turns out it's actually just a thing Albertans like to say a lot 'cause they like their meat all rare there.

I gnawed that fuckin' thing down to the bone pretty quick. He laughed and threw me another like I was a bear at the zoo, and, I'm ashamed to say, I ate that one right down, too.

"I'm impressed, kid!" he said, and he grinned and pulled out of the cowgirl, who he was fucking from behind by then, and made a "go to it" gesture at her ass.

The next thing I know I'm fucking the cowgirl from behind, totally bareback, of course. So, there's a tiny little blip of a blackout where I guess I made the decision to fuck her at the demand of this guy.

Then, I remember, I looked at her ass and I looked down at my dick. My T-shirt was stained with meat juice. It looked like I'd been shot. I suddenly had a vision of myself, from outside myself. What I looked like. I can still see that. See why I wish I had more blackouts?

Later, back at our motel, first time I told the story I was pretty proud of myself for pulling out and not continuing to fuck the girl. I was proud that I had realized this was a bad idea and had the presence of mind to stop it. But then when I finished telling the story, Giulietta looked so angry she almost looked sad. Her eyes were shining a little bit as she sarcastically slow clapped at me and said, "My hero." That's when I first started to realize I had kind of fucked up. I guess I'm still a fuckhead but I hope I never go quite so far down fuckhead alley as that again.

Oh, right, you wanted to know about the border crossing. Anyway, that's how fucked things were at Steerpunchers, just to give you an idea.

GIULIETTA CAETANO

HER HOUSE, TUCSON, ARIZONA, 2016

TOM CAME BURSTING OUT OF THE KITCHEN with his cum-drippin' dick hangin' out, covered in blood, including his face. What kind of blood? I do not want to know. He screamed, "We Gotta Get Outta This Place!" and jumped up on the bar. People cheered, and for a moment there was a hanging pause because, oh, man, he didn't know what he was going to do! The crowd didn't know what he was going to do! But we (his band) knew what he was going to do. We knew *exactly* what he was going to do.

Hey man, you can always count on Tom when it comes down to a moment like this: Tom will always find somewhere inappropriate to huck a piss.

I've seen him piss while driving the van so as not to have to stop, and seen him fumble the bottle, sprayin' urination around in a kind of piss fountain. I've been in hotels and private homes when Tom was around where I remember thinking, "Shit, we forgot to close all the drawers." He's even pissed in the vegetable drawers of several closed refrigerators at house parties I've attended, and once, in a full drunken state, he patiently picked the lock of a small safe in order to piss in it. DD said she sincerely regretted teaching him lock-picking after that. He'll piss out of a moving van, laughing;

he's pissed on the windows of businesses that wouldn't let us use the bathroom and on the windows of businesses that he loves dearly. The big picture window at Tuesday's is coated with a thin film of piss, much of which belongs to Tom. We were in Toronto at the NXNE music conference once and he started pissing in the middle of a traffic island. DD said, "Tom, you can't pee there!" and Tom just smiled and said, "Oh, no, actually you can! See?"

So I knew what he was going to do as soon as I saw him. Everybody else had to wait to find out.

I seriously think we could have kept working that place at least until the end of Stampede, but after DD talked Tom down from the bar and he slipped on some of his own piss but managed not to break anything — we headed straight back to the motel and we all were of the same mind that we really did "gotta get out of there."

TOM ABBOTT

KINGSTON'S SECOND OLDEST BAR, AFTER CLOSING, 2015

I KNEW THE FOOD POISONING WAS A JUDGMENT on me for what had been going on in the kitchen. Do I consider myself a rapist? No. Fuck. Was I some kind of accessory to some kind of chemical attack on those girls by the Man in White? Yeah, well, maybe, that's a bit more in the possible category there. Not legally. But I knew I'd done wrong. How do you make up for something like that? I never even knew those women's names. Who were they? Were they hookers? Were they just party girls, fucking for more coke? Fucked if I know. Hell, for all I know, one of them was the guy's wife. Maybe he was a Mormon and they were all his wives. If I saw them on the street today, I prob'ly wouldn't even recognize them, partly because women's faces are always changing. A lot of times I don't recognize a girl two years after the last time I saw her, and sometimes a girl will come up to me and claim to be the girl from one gig or party or festival or another, and I just have to take her word for it.

You could take out an ad in the paper, in the back of the *Calgary Sun* or Calgary Craigslist, I guess, saying, "if you were drugged or poisoned with booze in the kitchen at Steerpunchers bar and I fucked you when you were beyond capacity to say yes or no, I'm truly sorry.

I should have known I was doing wrong when I was doing it but I was super hammered and coked up and young and stupid and my libido was dialed up to eleven back then," but I'm not sure that would really be much of a help to that girl's feelings. Fuuuck.

Anyway, we were at the motel for just a few ticks of the second hand before that steak exploded inside of me. Like a biological weapon. Like a bacteria bomb. Like a scouring brush of hate for the entire human race.

GIULIETTA CAETANO

HER HOUSE, TUCSON, ARIZONA, 2016

TOM WAS A COMPLETE MESS. He started by saying his fingers felt numb, and then his face, and then he just started puking and shitting. That went on for, like, days, man. We talked about taking him to the hospital but he didn't want to go. He has some kind of superstition about that.

Any time he came to himself for a minute he would just return to the theme of "We Gotta Get Outta This Place," and in terms of "this place" being a pukey-shitty-smelling Motel 6 on the side of Deerfoot Trail, he had us all on board, absolutely.

We were holed up in that Motel 6 with a whole lot of coke from Steerpunchers and plenty of hard liquor, too, and nothing to do, so that's where I'd say most of the album was written. Tom had already thrown his songs into the repertoire so we just polished the arrangements of those, and DD had a song called "Edge of the World" that she seemed to just pull out of her ass, and that's where Jacob wrote "Constant Perpetual Wreck" and "Wasted Song." ("You're already gone, so this is just a wasted song." That song came to haunt me later.)

[Pause.]

All the while we were planning our next move, and Jacob really wanted to get to America. I was up for that. I wanted to see if our country music could cut it on the streets of the country it came from.

DD has this way of objecting to stuff where she doesn't really object. She just gently slips in her objections in some kind of positive, supportive statement. Like, she really is on your side looking out for your best interests, and she wants to be encouraging, but she's secretly hoping if she brings the problems with your thinking out into the light, you'll twig to it and change your mind. Like a breeze blows in through the window and you think it's all your idea.

She said stuff like, "Wow! That's gonna be fun. Should we take a look at a map and see how our route's gonna go here?" and, "I had no idea they didn't watch that part of the border. That's amazing. You'd think they'd be watching the whole thing with cameras or something," and also, "So, what happens if somebody does accidentally get caught? Do they still impound your van and auction it off? My dad used to get some amazing deals down at the border police auction in Blaine."

It's funny. That technique she has is the sort of thing that women and Indigenous people are more likely to take into account and white men will not hear at all. Tom and Jacob were kind of halfway between DD's world and the world of sonofabitch assholes. They could often hear what she was saying, but there were times when they would just switch back into being straight white guys who ran shit, especially if they had really got a tight hold of an idea they liked.

On this project, they did not hear any of DD's objections at all. They were on a mission from God. They said things like, "See, there's a difference between a fuckin' *undefended* border and an *unpatrolled* border," and then they'd nod sagely, like that pretty much explained it. All I can say is it seemed like a good idea at the drunk-and-high time.

Here was the plan: Jacob had a conviction, so he couldn't cross the border. So he and Tom would simply walk along the Milk River in the night. Just follow the Milk River, and, sooner than later, it would take them across the border.

Meanwhile, DD and me would go across the real official border with all the instruments and stuff in the van in the fairly early morning, then cut east and wait along the Milk with a pair of binoculars and pick them up when they inevitably intersected with us. We would pack sandwiches because they'd be hungry by the time we met up. That was the plan. Simple, huh? Simple and stupid.

TOM ABBOTT

KINGSTON'S SECOND OLDEST BAR, AFTER CLOSING, 2015

I KNOW I'M NOT EXACTLY A GENIUS about living now, but, boy oh boy, sometimes I wonder how it is I survived my twenties with all my extremities intact.

Once I felt strong enough to walk, the girls set me and Jacob down beside the river in the national park around there. We each had a backpack with water and some energy bars in it, and a couple flashlights, which we didn't plan to use except in an emergency because that might draw eyes our way. We wore our darkest clothes. It was the height of summer so it was pretty warm even at night.

We walked along. It was beautiful. There was a half moon that kept going in and out of cloud. The trees were a little smaller and scrubbier than I was used to; they didn't provide great cover. You had to walk carefully along the rock or you'd stumble.

I still felt weaker than I wanted to admit. I must have lost twenty pounds from the steak of retribution. I had a sense of hope about crossing the border, though. I really felt like it was going to put a line under or over every stupid asshole thing I'd been doing up to then, and give me a fresh start. I know Jacob felt the same. Or maybe he was just trying to escape from thinking about the girl and the kid he'd left behind.

Strangely, we felt pretty good, even though I had little faint moments where I had to stop and just breathe a couple times. Had to concentrate on not falling when I stepped on loose rock.

And then we came to the border, and that's when we knew in our hearts how fuckin' stupid we were.

See, we'd been working on the idea that a huge, undisputed, friendly border might be a patrolled border but it wouldn't be a fenced border. And if it *was* fenced, well, as long as it wasn't walled or barbwired or anything, Jacob and DD and I had hopped a lot of trains, gotten into a lot of things we weren't supposed to get into. We felt like we could beat anything that wasn't actually a guarded fence. We didn't figure on the lights.

Fuck, those lights! Bright, bright, brighter-than-a-movie-shoot lights, big towers of them looming over the river valley.

We lay on the ground, peering from over a rock. We knew we were fucked, but we kept trying to think our way through the problem.

Jacob said, "Get out your watch; let's time these lights. We'll run when they turn off."

We did that for a while. I guess they'd thought of that, 'cause we lay there for, I dunno, two hours, and there was no pattern we could find in it. It was just fucking random.

Fuck me, is what I thought. *How can this be?* I thought I was fated to cross this border so I could slither my old asshole skin off behind me. But now we were being stymied.

Jacob said, "We can't give up that easy, you fucking pussy. We'll go in the river. We'll just grab some stray branches and bob along and they won't be able to see us. Hell, we don't actually know if anybody's even watching, right?"

Well, I wasn't going to be the one to pussy out on something, so I agreed, even though I wasn't too sure about his logic there.

But once we were down there in the muddy water, crouched and wade-swimming and fuckin' cold, I started to think. I was looking at the dirty back of Jacob's neck. The lights had come on a couple of times, and we had ducked under water. I was wondering about the current. Could it carry us away? Could it drown us? Could we really get down past the lights like this? And I started to construct a new version of my story of getting across the border and leaving my old jerk self behind.

I thought, *Hey, maybe I've already suffered enough, after puking and shitting my guts out for almost a week, and now crawling through the mud and probably getting hypothermia. Maybe this border is impassable, and that's, like, a symbol of how I can't leave myself behind by crossing some fucking man-made, political border. Maybe by turning back, and going deeper into myself, and maybe stopping doing cocaine and meth, and leaving tequila and whisky and sticking with only beer, I could make that leap into a new phase of my life without drowning or winding up in fucking Guantánamo Bay.*

That's what I thought. After we ducked under for the fourth time, and we came up, I put my hand on Jacob's shoulder. He turned. I looked him deep in the eye.

"Brother, this is fucked. Let's go back."

He just looked right back into me. The moonlight caught him, and he suddenly looked like a little kid. He looked like he was going to cry. Looking back now, I guess that although I had created a new story to make going back all right for me, I hadn't really made a new story for him, and to him, this was his last chance to start again. Now, in his mind, he was going to have to be resigned to staying how he was. I should have helped him more during that period. I should have helped him work his way through, to become a more mature, together guy. But he could be such an asshole that it sort of discouraged you from doing that. And I guess I kinda had my hands full with myself.

He didn't say anything. He just nodded and turned around. I've never seen anybody look more sad.

GIULIETTA CAETANO

HER HOUSE, TUCSON, ARIZONA, 2016

WE LOADED UP THE VAN WITH instruments and sandwiches and a couple of fancy mountain bikes that some rich guy had given us as a joke back at the bar, and we dropped the boys off on the side of the road. I must have asked Tom, like, five times if he truly was up for it, because Jacob started to get pretty touchy. It's just that Tom didn't look too good. He wasn't puking or shitting himself anymore, he was just having to take little breaks and lean on things like newspaper boxes and lampposts. He didn't order his usual car-bomb coffee (an espresso dunked into a medium drip coffee); he had tea. Tom drinking tea — that was messed up.

The fifth time I asked him if he was okay, he looked me in the eye with that sincere hound-dog look that Tom will do when he's feeling full of soul, and said, "This is something I have to do, okay? If I make it, or if I don't make it, it doesn't matter. I just have to do this. Can you understand that?"

I said, "Oh my God, Tom, have we watched *Red Dawn* a few too many times as a child, maybe?" and he laughed and told me to fuck off.

We checked with each other one more time about the plan. Walk down the Milk River and we'll meet you. We'll have the sandwiches.

We breezed through the border no problem. I've never seen DD have trouble at a border checkpoint. In fact, border guards love her. She's just so nonchalant and happy to be driving. It's infectious.

"And what's your reason for crossing today, ladies?"

"No big reason, we just thought we'd go down to America for a few days and see what kinda trouble we could get into." The big guy with the automatic pistol on his belt just laughed and waved us through. I'm serious.

Nobody had cellphones at that point. I feel old telling you about this but in fact, at one point having a cellphone was a total bourgeois thing to do. Only yuppies and wannabes had cellphones. Real people would not even, like, touch them. I know that seems silly now but, anyway, we didn't have cellphones so we had no way to reach the boys.

So, we took a left and headed uphill until we reached a promontory that overlooked the Milk River. And then we sat there for a while. DD had some binoculars.

And we sat there and we sat there and we sat there.

Then we got out and we sat on the hood of the van, and we ate some sandwiches. But we saved a sandwich each for the boys, because we knew they were going to get hungry if they ever got to us.

Then she looked at me and I looked at her, and she said, "I'm bored."

So we went in the back of the van and fucked. I didn't get off because I was nervous about the whole situation.

Then we came out and sat on the hood of the van and smoked so we wouldn't get hungry and eat the boys' sandwiches.

Another hour or two went by and we said, "Aw, hell with it," and started eating the boys' sandwiches.

That's when a big pickup truck came up the road. A man got of out of the truck in a plaid shirt and a 10-gallon hat and walked toward us. I noticed the gun rack on his truck.

He didn't say, "Hello, ladies," or, "What's up? Are you okay there?" or anything like that. He just walked up and put his hands on his hips and said, “If you got B.C. plates in these parts, yer up to no good.”

“We’re just having sam-witches,” said DD, brightly. But he wasn’t buying it. He just walked back to his truck and drove away.

Oh shit, is what I thought.

TOM ABBOTT

KINGSTON'S SECOND OLDEST BAR, AFTER CLOSING, 2015

WE DIDN'T TALK AT ALL AS WE TRUDGED out of that river valley, cold, muddy, tired, still half sick, feeling sicker. I stumbled a couple times going back up those rocky inclines, but Jacob didn't turn around. I don't think he didn't care that I'd fallen; I think he was just so far in his head that he didn't notice.

I bet we looked fuckin' charming as we stood there by the side of the road with our thumbs out in the thin morning light. I sure-as-shit wouldn't have picked us up. Our external appearance matched our fucked-up, filthy, unredeemed internal lives pretty good.

A big, deluxe Peterbilt with North Dakota plates stopped for us and it was a couple guys in full hunting camos. There was a gun rack on either side of the cab with a big old wood stock rifle of some kind on one side and a sawed-off shotgun on the other. Sawed-off shotguns make me nervous. I feel they only have one purpose.

Those guys weren't talking much either.

I tried to strike the right note of friendliness.

"Well, fellas, thanks a lot for picking us up. I don't know what we would have done without you."

One of them grunted. They just watched the road.

"Well, we don't want to be any trouble. If you can just drop us off at the nearest town with a pay phone in it, we'd really appreciate it."

"That's Lorris. About an hour from here. You wanna go to Lorris?"

"Um, sure. That sounds fine. That first beer in Lorris is gonna taste pretty good."

Another grunt.

Jacob has a fuckin' amazing instinct for zeroing in on the trouble in any situation and just poking it right in the tender spot.

"So, boys, what are we haulin'?"

Silence.

Then the driver said to his buddy, "I don't know, Bob. What *are* we haulin'?"

Bob didn't turn to look at nobody. Just kept staring straight ahead. Said, "Meat."

Nobody said anything after that.

GIULIETTA CAETANO

HER HOUSE, TUCSON, ARIZONA, 2016

EVENTUALLY THEY CAME FOR US. First we saw clouds of dust in the distance. I said, "You think those are trucks?"

And DD said, "Yup."

And I said, "Do you think they're coming for us?"

And she said, "I don't see anything else around except a couple of cows. So, I think they're coming for us."

She didn't squeeze my hand. She just looked cool. Unconcerned. Smoking calmly. I felt braver seeing her cool like that. I was kind of losing it.

"What if they strip-search us? What if they cavity search us? I don't think I could handle that. That's too fucked up." I got up and moved around. DD stayed still and smoked steadily.

I felt really scared. We'd all heard about the shitty things the border police do to people, how there's no law at the border. I was kind of thinking aloud, freaking out about it all. DD just sat still and smoked, looking off into the distance.

It turned out to be nothing too agro. Nobody pulled any firearms out. Just a cop-type car from the border patrol. "Okay, ladies, let's get you back to your vehicle. We're going to be escorting you back to the border now." They didn't put a weird stamp on our passports or anything.

Then when DD got past the border, she pulled the van over. She didn't look at me; she stared straight out at the road and said, "Don't mind me, I'm just going into the back to do something for a while. Be good to go soon."

She climbed into the back and got under some blankets we had under the back bench. She hid her face, and just stayed there for about two hours. About halfway into that, I called back and said, "Hey. Are you okay?" and I went back to just ... pat her or something.

"I'm okay!" she said in this weird, shaky, high-pitched voice.

"Are you sure?"

"Yeah, but is it okay if you don't come near me for a little bit? Definitely don't touch me, okay?"

"Okay."

I just sat and waited. After a couple of hours, she came outta there and sat in the driver seat. She took a deep breath, turned the ignition, and put it in gear. She didn't say anything about that, ever.

We drove to find a pay phone and called DD's dad. We had arranged for him to be the communications hub because he rarely moved from the kitchen table in Port anymore. "They're in Lorris. I don't think they're doing so great, though. It's a dry town."

We got to the motel in Lorris, the Colonial Inn, and there they were looking pretty shaky, lying on the bed watching *Deliverance* on TV.

"Well, that's gotta qualify as one of the dumbest things I've ever done," Jacob said.

DD slapped him, you know, playfully, on the side of the head. DD was the only person I ever saw Jacob let get away with anything like that. "Oh, I wouldn't say that. You've done plenty of dumber things than that, buddy."

TOM ABBOTT

KINGSTON'S SECOND OLDEST BAR, AFTER CLOSING, 2015

BY THE TIME WE FINALLY GOT BACK TO VICTORIA, we were all in fuckin' sad shape. G and DD took off immediately in the van for California. They were both, of course, drinking beer as a constant through-line, and doing coke whenever they could get a hold of it. We had made a stop in Lethbridge, where we had tried to simultaneously record an album and quit meth and speed and coke, as a band, after the failed attempt at crossing the border. The idea was to go on ginseng and, I don't know, tiger balm or whatever, but when we listened to the playback at mixing time, the result was pathetically slow. We sounded great as a band when we were going fuckin' full tilt, but if you slowed it all down to walking speed, you could really hear how pitchy our vocals got and how often Jacob's banjo was out of whack because he hit the strings so hard his instrument just wouldn't stay in tune. So we got a hold of a fuckin' Antarctica of coke and just went at 'er and did the whole thing in thirty-six hours straight. All fifteen songs, all tracks, recorded and mixed. Which we never released. Which is a shame. When we were done, there was nothing to do but go back to Victoria. That felt like a funeral. Especially for Jacob.

Jacob was the worst. He would just not be seen for days. He would go back to Amy, scare the shit out of everybody in the house, and then leave. He looked like a concentration camper. I mean, not just 'cause he was thin and dark-eyed. He looked scared. Even when he was super angry, he looked scared at the same time.

I was still carrying the shit from what I'd done at fuckin' Steerpunchers. I felt dirty. Like, when you realize you are not one of the good guys in the movie anymore. You are one of the bad guys.

The only sort of worthwhile thing I was doing was every now and then I had to come over to Amy's and run Jacob out of the house. At first I was trying to defuse things, just saying, "Hey brother, I'm achin' for a beer. Come on out to Tuesday's; it's on me," that kinda thing. But I saw the way the little boy looked when he was around. That kid looked like kids should not look. Looked worried. Looked serious. Then on later visits I was like, "Okay bud, we gotta go," and I was just tired of it. He threw furniture through the windows, he punched holes in the wall. He definitely tossed Amy around a few times. Eventually I was in the position where I had to gear myself up because I knew I had to actually fuckin' headlock him and drag him out on the lawn. I tried to be gentle with him. He was my friend. He was just in a very bad space and he needed to not be there. I wasn't trying to hurt him. It was fucked up. It didn't make me feel like a hero.

Then one time I came over, I didn't even know DD was back in town. I had heard she was living down in Cali with G. By this point I had it down to a science. I told Amy to call these dickheads Jacob had been hanging out with. I figured if I released him from the headlock on the front lawn and his stupid new friends were there waiting for him, he'd just climb in and take off to party some more.

So, yeah, I'm hauling him out the front door. He braces himself on the door jamb, shouting, "I'm just trying to *talk* to the mother of my *child* here!" and I had to use my workboot to kick his boot out of the way. Then I toss him on to the unmowed grass. He's lying there. "You are not my friend," he says.

Then his new buds pull up in an old painted-over city-works van they must have got at an auction or something.

It's right about this time DD pulls up in this awesome old yellow Ford truck with blue California plates. I'm like, "Wow, DD's back. That was fast." Jacob picks himself up and ambles over to the passenger seat of the asshole van.

DD steps out of her truck, which is still running. Idling a little rich. I'm sitting on the front step watching. Jacob's settling into the front seat of the asshole van. The window is rolled down.

"Hey, asshole!" DD is heading toward the van. I notice she's got a bit of a limp. But she's moving pretty quick.

Jacob kind of looks at her. "What's yer problem?" and she fucking launches herself at him. In a single step she's on the running board of the van and just fucking *whaling* on Jacob's face with her right hand. It's a textbook fucking street punch. Grasping the inside of the door through the window for purchase, it's like, rotate the whole body, cock fist, WHAM! in the face, rotate, cock fist, WHAM! in the face. Fucking at least four of five times. And she's just doing the classic up-volume of her voice with each swing, like, "Don't you (here comes the punch) *ever* let me see you (here comes the punch) *come* round here again! And if I *ever* hear you touch her or the baby *again*, I know people, and you *know* who I'm talkin' about, and I will call them, and you'll be *fucking. Dead.*" I mean she just fucking nailed him.

She leaped off the running board and staggered a little bit with the weak leg, and just screamed, "*Get the fuck outta here!!*" and that van didn't have to be told twice. Those tweakers were not going to mess with her. They were gone, and it did keep Jacob away for, like, years.

Later we were in Amy's living room. DD was on the couch with her right hand in a bucket of ice and a beer and a smoke in her left. Amy was giving her a haircut.

DD put the beer down and came over and looked me in the eye and said, "Hey, buddy. How's things going in there?" She meant, like, in me, inside my head.

I nodded at her scraped, swollen right paw. "How's things with you?"

"I'm okay." She smiled. "Just needed to get a few things out of my system, you know. I feel a lot better now." She winked at me, like she'd just been out on the lawn playing skittles instead of beating a man twice her height half to death with her bare hands. "But you seem kinda low."

I said, "Yeah, well, I miss feeling all right. I miss feeling like the scrappy underdog. I miss myself like I thought I was." Or some shit like that. She said, "You playin' music at all?"

I mumbled something about not leaving the house much.

"Well," she said, "if you can drag your sorry ass down to the Hullaballoo on Sunday we could maybe play a couple tunes."

I told her how I didn't deserve music. How I had betrayed music. She just nodded and punched me lightly on the shoulder.

But then I kept feeling shittier. It was a downward spiral. For weeks. I'd actually set myself up to hang myself from an exercise bar thing for doorways that I'd got from Canadian Tire. Wasn't sure if it was gonna hold me, but I was all set to try. I mean, I was ready to die. Then, the day I was gonna do it, just as I was sorta getting ready, I just kinda thought, *Well, maybe I'll just go for a little walk, out in Victoria in the autumn, just to say goodbye to things.*

And then I was walking around in the fall air. The trees were all the pretty way they are in the fall and all. Even the yellow and red leaves mushing up in the storm drains looked kinda gold and ruby red. It was all so lovely, that it made me just think, *This world. This world is just too beautiful for you, you piece of shit,* and I sort of wandered through the park next to Crystal Pool, and kids were playing and shouting. These kids were swinging on the swings, and they had all this joy on their faces, and it really made me feel even more like the world would be a safer, better place without jerks like me in it. But then I did sort of wander over to Amy's house.

DD let me in, she said, "Hi, buddy. Haven't seen you for a while. I was just going to go over and check on ya to see if you're still breathing." I mean, she knew. She didn't have to be told. And she welcomed me in. And I went up to Amy who was drinking tea and reading in the kitchen, and said, "Hey, can I maybe hold your guitar?" and she nodded. I played one of the ones we used to play on the street together, that Woody Guthrie song "I Ain't Got No Home in This World Anymore."

I looked at DD and said, "I guess I wasn't the best person back in Alberta there."

She already had the fiddle in her hand. "Your high E is a little flat."

We played a couple more tunes.

I started to feel a bit better. We tried a couple of my own old songs; it turned out I still knew them fine.

That Sunday I started playing them at the Hullaballoo Open Mic at Tuesday's. And I started doing mostly okay. Better. Going to the Dutch Bakery. Having a coffee. I could read a book again.

I mean I started to get better. I'm not perfect. I'm no angel. I still occasionally, when I'm maybe tired or waited too long to eat or something, I just kind of remember how I fuckin' despise myself and I feel like I have to do something to myself to make things even up a bit … and I'll sip a beer on a Thursday night and wake up Monday morning in some small town in Quebec, freezing wet from melted snow in somebody's living room with the wood stove gone out and scrapes all over me and wishing I had no idea what happened. But I am way better than I was, most of the time. I get by, and I don't wanna hang myself. DD did that for me. That's what I want you to understand about DD.

GIULIETTA CAETANO

HER HOUSE, TUCSON, ARIZONA, 2016

LOOK: IT'S ALL PRETTY BAD. We were all pretty bad. Music had saved us, and then we had let the music down, somehow. The death of the band hit us all pretty hard. And I was messed up about some stuff that had happened with a relative when I was a kid. Okay, I'm not going into that here. And that's not an excuse.

I could sit here and say, "Huh, I don't know why DD went back up to Vic a few months after we got to Santa Cruz," but I'm trying to live my life with some honesty and some transparency, and I'm just going to take ownership of what happened.

We took the ferry across from Tsawwassen to Swartz Bay, dropped Jacob and Tom off in Victoria, handed them all the cash we'd made on the tour in exchange for their shares of the van, and we drove right onto the Port Angeles ferry. We were done. We were starting a new life, together.

That night we slept in each other's arms in the van, somewhere just north of Portland. Next day I got my mom to wire us a few hundred dollars and we picked it up in a Western Union in Eugene.

That got us down to Santa Cruz. It's more gentrified now, but back then it was still largely kinda hippy and surfer-ey. We started busking on the streets, and we were making some money at it. We'd split a twenty-sixer of Southern Comfort every day, and we slept in the van and moved it when rent-a-cops came along. We had no home, but we were home to each other.

We got enough money to move into a motel that offered weekly rates, not too far from the beach. Then we got enough to get a second-hand surfboard that we shared.

We told each other that we were in love. I felt in love at the time, but, looking back, maybe I just wanted to own DD, or own her luck, or whatever it is about her. There was *something* about her that I couldn't quite pull off, and I couldn't figure out what it was. We both let our hair grow out, and we looked pretty alike, although I'm a bit taller. I was maybe kind of living an impression of DD at the time. I was trying to *get* DD somehow.

I know I'm pretty. I have a dark beauty. That's just a fact. I've always been a girl who girls and guys want to get with. I'm actually technically better looking than her, if you saw a photo of the two of us. But it was always DD who drew people in to try to make a spiritual connection. It was always DD who people wanted to really know. And there was something about me at the time … I didn't have that. And it showed in the difference between how I played and how she played. I wanted to be in the moment, but she *was* in the moment. She was the moment. Like the song goes, I saw the crescent, and she saw the whole of the moon. And I was jealous of that. I admit that to myself now. That's progress, right?

One day, the van gave out. I was driving it when it happened. It was the transmission. And DD always kind of rode me about how I shifted the gears. She said I changed gears like an elderly farmer on an elderly tractor, whatever that means. She said she meant it affectionately, but it still bugged me. She had a special relationship with vehicles, too. So when the van broke when I was driving it, she took me under the van and showed me what had failed, and she implied that it was the way I shifted the gears that had ground it down — not in so many words, but it was clear what she was thinking. The tension between us was getting up there.

Then she insisted we needed to get another vehicle right away. She spotted this photocopied ad on the corkboard at some surf shop for this old yellow Ford truck, and she insisted we go look at it. The ad said it wasn't running, but she said her "motor sense" told her we had to look at it. I didn't understand why we would go look at a truck that wasn't running. She said if a truck that good was running, we wouldn't be able to afford it.

We go to the place, and it's one of these collective houses where young surfer hippies all live together. The dude was there, classic dirty-blond surfer with dreads and this tall, skinny blond woman with tan lines on her back. She had dreads, too. DD calls white people's dreads "lice mittens." I got the vibe off her that she wasn't really a poor hippy, that she had some family money or something that was supporting them. Just the way she held herself, and she had a really gorgeous Guatemalan craft bag.

The truck was in the driveway. It was old and dirty, but it wasn't rusty. I could see that. Dude said, "I don't know what the deal is. It just stopped running. I had a mechanic friend look at it and he said it would cost a couple grand to repair. So I'm just, like, what the fuck, you know?"

DD went and looked it over. No expression on her face. Poker face. Looked all around the interior, looked under the thing. Then she got in and popped the hood.

She hopped out and hauled herself up to stand on the front bumper and had a look at the engine. I saw her eyes widen just for a tiny second. The dude and dudette didn't see it. Then she put the hood down again.

"Well, it's pretty buggered up. But I like it. How much you want for it? You said five hundred? We'll give you three hundred cash money today. Right now, and we'll pay for the tow, if you call the truck."

That was good enough for the trustafarian girl, who just wanted the thing gone from the driveway. The dude shrugged. I think he was pretty baked.

I was like, "I don't know, man. Why do we want to spend our last cash on a truck that doesn't run?"

DD said, "I'm just sentimental about yellow trucks. If you love me, baby, will you let me have it?" She said this in a kind of dumb girly voice but widened her eyes at me meaningfully. It kinda irritated me, mostly.

As we waited for the tow truck, the girl was already connecting with DD. "You guys should come over this weekend. We have these awesome potlucks where we network with people about building the scene. I make a wicked vegan coconut pie. We're just trying to make a safe space where people can share their truth. We all need to play our role in evolving toward a better world, right?" or whatever. But I could tell she was really saying, "I would totally love for you to do me on my futon under my parachute awning while my boyfriend is off surfing."

The tow truck came and took us back to the motel. I'd paid the girl, and now paid the truck driver with pretty much our last stash of cash. DD lit a smoke and waited for the tow truck to go out of sight.

With her cigarette hanging off her lip, she said, "C'mere, you gotta see this."

She threw the hood up, propped it on the rod, and pointed to the engine. "See anything there that strikes you as odd?"

I looked. DD had taught me how to look at cars. It mostly involves turning off the voice that says, "I don't know anything about cars," and taking a good look to see if anything looks melted or busted or burned or strangely loose. "It kinda looks like maybe those wires aren't connected to anything."

"Right. They should be hooked into these holes, where the cylinders are. But they're just hanging higgledy-piggledy. Know what's in the holes instead?"

I took a look.

She reached in, and grabbed one of them.

"Pencils. HB pencils," she said, laughing. "Somebody must've wanted to teach that dude a lesson or something. Now, let's see what happens when we take all eight pencils out and plug these suckers back in."

She quickly popped everything into place and handed me eight yellow pencils.

Then she jumped in the driver's seat, pumped the gas a couple times, and turned the key. The thing started just like that. Who puts pencils in somebody's truck engine?

The car ran smooth. It was a fucking mint vintage truck, worth at least ten grand to a collector, minimum, man, minimum, and we'd bought it for three hundred bucks plus a twenty-dollar towing charge. And somehow, instead of feeling like, "Hey! We scored! Go us!" I was, like, somehow totally pissed off by this. I can't explain it.

I was like, "Wow. Somebody totally scammed those people. We should tell them. We should give it back to them. It's not honest."

DD looked at me like I had just turned into a duck-billed platypus. "Sorry?"

"We should give it back."

"Why?"

"It's not right. We ripped them off."

"Baby, the Plush Monster don't run no more. We are fucking stranded. We need this truck way more than they do. You said yourself on the ride here they looked rich."

"Rich or poor, it's not right."

It takes a lot to make DD darken. But this was doing it. I was getting to her. She said, "Oh, I'm sorry, I thought I was talking to the girl who suck-siphoned a full tank of gas out of a Lincoln in a Denny's parking lot in Brandon, Manitoba. The girl who stole nail polish from the drugstore in Kindersley. The girl who jumped over the front desk and grabbed a fifty-dollar bill from the till of a motel in Nanaimo. The girl who —" I just yelled at her to *shut up, shut up, shut up*.

She shut up. But then she wouldn't talk to me for an hour or so.

After a while I said sorry, sorry, sorry. She accepted my apology and let me hug her but she didn't hug back. I said if we were gonna get rid of the good ol' Plush Monster, maybe we could spend one more night in it, for old times' sake. She said okay.

I went and got a bunch of beer.

We sat in the parking lot of our motel, drinking beer and hotboxing the Plush Monster. DD found a full mickey of vodka somewhere in the back between all the old cushions, and we drank that, too.

I don't know what happened to set me off. She said something, and then I said something. Then she said something. We'd been lying there on the back velour bench together, and I had been resting my legs on her lap. She was kind of wedged into the plush corner.

So we started fighting …

[Pause.]

And when it was over, she was like, "I need you to get me to a hospital."

[Pause.]

Okay, I'm done talking here. That's enough.

AMY WILLIAMS

HER KITCHEN, FERNWOOD NEIGHBOURHOOD, VICTORIA, 2014

THE NIGHT WE ACTUALLY GOT TOGETHER was kind of intense.

It was Rosalyn Knight's album release show at Lucky Bar. I hadn't been out at night, without the baby, for eighteen months. He was almost two. I'd been fucking entombed in baby-land for literally ever. Wyatt had finally been sleeping through the night most of the time, and I had been able to sing backup on Rosalyn's record, at Sea of Shit Studios. She had held the kid while I did my track, which was something she never did. She claims to be allergic to children — they make her break out in tiny little whining hives, she says. That's one of the things I always found so refreshing about her — her open dislike for children. I mean, all of society is set up *as if* everybody hated kids, but Rosalyn is one of the few women with the courage to just say, "No, I prefer to be a barren, childless, empty-wombed old maid, thank you." She really says stuff like that.

Rosalyn called me and asked me to come out and sing at the release show, and I said, "Sure, *you* call my mother and talk her into babysitting," because my mother was the only person besides me that Wyatt would allow himself to get put to bed by. Rosalyn just said okay and called back half an hour later. "It's set. Report for duty at 6:00 p.m., Agent Williams."

I couldn't believe it. But at five o'clock sharp there was Mother at the door, carrying toys, extra wipes, and lots of judgment for my housecleaning skills and choice of outfit.

I was both super fucking happy about finally being let out of baby prison and super fucking anxious, wondering if I even remembered how to fucking operate in a live-music bar setting.

I hadn't been really drinking at all for the past year, just smoking a few hits off a pocket pipe when I needed to slow my brain down so I could play hide-and-seek for hours with a small person who always hid in the same spot behind the couch. So I was a bit of a lightweight, alcoholically speaking, at that point in my life. But like I say, I was super fucking anxious, and so I had picked up a cheap bottle of red wine in Rosalyn's honour just to have a glass before I set out for the night.

I had to change my dress a couple times as I was getting ready, because I kept seeing myself in the mirror and thinking, *Is* that *your final answer for what you wanna look like on your only night out ever?* So, getting ready took a little longer than I had time-budgeted for and by the time I left the house I'd had more like three glasses of wine. I kidded myself that my mom hadn't been watching how much I'd drank.

I walked the twenty-five minutes to the hall. I didn't want to spend drinks money on a cab. By then my feet were kind of hurting from my heels, so when I got to the bar and the bartender was so glad to see me after all this time that he offered me a tequila shot, I figured it was essential to deal with the pain from my feet. One of my blisters had already burst but I looked awesome.

I was late for sound check but of course they were still setting up the snakes and mic stands so I went backstage where Rosalyn had a big box of wine going and she said, "Amy! Welcome to sound-wait again! Have a glass of box wine. We're working on our coordinated dance steps."

We worked on the shuffling backup-singer choreography for about half an hour while we waited to check, and I was careful just to nurse the plastic glass of box wine, which wasn't too hard because it was kinda nasty. "Just the right over-notes of blood and metal," as Rosalyn put it.

Now I was feeling pretty great. And sound check was probably the best performance I'd given in years. I had the dance steps, I had the part (I'd had nothing to do but practise in the house for weeks so I was goddamn ready), and I had just the right blood-alcohol level for a worry-free performance. Sound check was fucking wicked. Then the Danger Time began.

Danger Time is that period between sound check and performance when there's fuck all to do but pass the time before you get on and play. Road dog musicians are usually supergood at foosball and pool and darts and pinball, all those shitty games that're sitting there in the bar for people to play while they wait for the next thing to happen. I was a little rusty at foosball, but when I was playing pinball, a gamed called *Getaway*, DD showed up. I was really in the zone, winning extra balls, getting the bonus multi-balls, everything. I was on a roll.

DD almost never shows up for sound check. She hates the *doosh! doosh! doosh!* of the kick drum being checked over and over. She hates the attitude of most sound guys. She hates to wait. It's understood that if you want DD in your band, you better forget about worrying too much about sound check. I've seen some band leaders really wring their hands over that — you included, Geoff Berner, but you know very well that she's right — if the tech is any good, DD'll sound good when she's ready to play, and if not, then no amount of fucking checking will help anyway.... Okay well, we'll have to agree to disagree about that. I know it drives Mykola crazy, too.

Anyway, I was fucking rocking out on the *Getaway* machine and suddenly there was DD at my side. "Shit, you never told me you could play pinball like that. Look at you go," she said, and whistled. And I just kind of had this out-of-nowhere rush of arousal, like getting hit by a tropical breeze or something. I was like, "Damn. I gotta figure out a way to fuck this girl." Sorry, that's just my, like, internal dialogue. Externally I was playing it cool. Like, "Yeah, I'm pretty good at the silver ball. I'm cool."

I could tell that I was kind of getting her going. She was like, "Can I get you a drink, Pinball Wizard?" and I wasn't gonna say no to that, partly just because I was close to broke and I wouldn't have turned down a free drink from Hitler at that point in my life. I decided to switch it up and asked for a gin and tonic, because I didn't want to get sleepy before the show and those things tend to wake me up a little. It's the fizz of the bubbles, or the lemon wedge, or something.

I drank that G and T (which I suspect was a double, it's always hard to tell with those) as I fucking ranked out on the pinball machine. Then me and DD went outside and I took a couple of hits off her hash pipe in the alley, and I just kind of smouldered at her and I think she got the message. She sort of smirked and raised her eyebrows at me.

By then I was really doing super great. I was a bit drunk, a bit high, I was free from having to take care of the baby every waking and half-waking moment, and I checked myself in the mirror in the ladies' room and I looked smoking hot. I would have done me, for sure. My burst blister was no longer bugging me, and I was singing my backup for practice, "Doom, sha-la-la, Doom, sha-la-la." I started looking for a guitar backstage because I wanted to jam with DD on a song I'd been working on at home and I was feeling creative as hell.

On my way to backstage, I had to navigate the main bar area. I ran into this couple I barely knew and they seemed so happy to see me that I would have felt rude not talking with them. The place was starting to fill up. The lady of the couple was dressed all in green with a vintage green frock and green stockings; she had orange hair and she said she was going to be the Green Party candidate for North Island. I talked about the Maa-nulth First Nations from around there and she nodded, and her guy said that sadly, he felt like since the Makah nation had started whaling again, what with whales being sentient beings, it felt like white environmentalists had become the new First Nations, in a way, so I threw what was left of my G and T in his face and skipped merrily backstage, looking for the boxed wine.

The boxed wine was gone, but Brody had brought a bunch of Lucky Lager and a big garbage can of ice. I guess it must have been summer and he had his roofing pay, otherwise there's no way he could have bought all that beer up front.

When your throat is dry from smoking a bowl, you can really appreciate a cold, crisp lager. Even Lucky Lager if it's just cold enough — and Brody knew to keep that lager cold, so it was perfect.

DD was nowhere to be found, so I sat there and shot the shit with Brody and Rosalyn. Just me and a couple of my fellow musicians, just, y'know, talkin' about the most important thing in the world — music. Not baby sleeping and potty training tips, or when to stop breastfeeding, none of that Mommy shit.

We talked about Roger Miller and to what degree he had formal jazz training and whether that was evident in the song "Dang Me."

We talked about the best way, in a live performance, to deliver Loretta Lynn's song "Fist City," as in when and how often and in what manner to flourish your fists when you're telling women to stay away from your man if they don't wanna go to Fist City, and whether it was better to have an open tuning on the guitar, so both hands could be free to fist as the chord rang.

We talked about whether Brody could convincingly cover it as a straight white man himself, at which point Brody began to mince around like a "lady," who somehow became the Lady Captain of a *Star Trek* space vessel who demanded that Mister La Forge flog her bottom with a rolled-up copy of *Tiger Beat* magazine, and alternated between screaming, "Whip me, Mister La Forge! *Yes*!" and a full lyrical performance of "Fist City" followed by a screamingly obscene S&M enactment of "You've Never Been This Far Before" by Conway Twitty. Rosalyn and I were rolling on the floor laughing, and DD walked backstage as I was begging Brody to tell his Pee-wee Herman/Hitler joke, which he told with great aplomb, and then DD said, "Well, the opening act has been off the stage for half an hour … maybe we ought to play." Which seemed odd to me, since DD was traditionally never the one to point to her watch, you know? I took that as a sign that I had maybe strayed into the unprofessional zone. But Rosalyn didn't seem bothered. "Welp, they can't start the show without us, can they?"

Then we did the show. At the time I was doing it, it felt fantastic. Looking back on it, it was probably *fine*. My plan was just to nurse my one Lucky Lager throughout the whole set, but when I picked it up to take it onstage, it was warming up and almost dead, so I had to grab another one. Then after the first song some secret admirer of Rosalyn's sent tequila shots up to the stage on a tray, one for each band member. You can't say no to that when the whole entire band is doing a ceremonial shot. That's camaraderie, that's band solidarity, you know? Yeah, you know what that's all about. Later I saw Cole Dixon hanging around the back of the hall wearing thick Clark Kent glasses, and I thought, *Hey, weird. Doesn't he live in Edmonton?* I think he was the secret tequila admirer.

Looking back on that now, it's funny 'cause I've always been like, *Why did I go so off that night?* I didn't have *that* much to drink, but now that I tell it, just give me a sec, can I look over your notes and see exactly how many drinks I'm up to in this story? …

Looks like nine, maybe ten. Depending on how much gin splashed in that guy's face. Plus the marijuana. Okay. Well, that makes a little more sense then. I had thought of myself as mainly just nursing drinks, but I guess I nursed a lot of drinks there. That's more of an explanation for what happened after that than I had really considered.

I checked in with people after, and everybody said that my singing stayed good. I don't think they all would have just *said* that.

I mean Brody, Rosalyn, DD, the others, they fuckin' live for the music, and they've all had me back playing at their gigs. So it can't have been that bad. I mean, the show was fucking fantastic, actually. Everybody played great. Rosalyn can sometimes go a little off, too, I mean, nobody's perfect and I'd rather be at an *off* Rosalyn show than an *on* anybody-else show. But she was totally on that night. Every little between-song remark, every interaction with the crowd, and the songs, of course. Those songs. Those songs were like she was reading my diary. Except with clever wordplay. And I don't keep a diary.

So that's why I was moved, somewhere around the tenth amazing song, to step up in front of the crowd with my microphone and just, you know, *testify* about my love for this woman, Rosalyn Knight. Do I remember the speech? Sure I do. Later in the night is a little patchy. But the speech is crystal clear in my memory for sure, because I guess I'd been writing it in my mind for, like, weeks before the show. I can't do it exactly. But it was like,

"Ladies and germs, just a second, wait, wait, wait, just give me a moment here …

"Ladies and germs, *this woman. Right here*. This woman is my fucking hero. You don't *know.* Well, some of you do. I worship this woman. The songs! And just look at her. With her raven hair, her awesome thrift-store dress, her awesome black guitar that she plays like nobody's business. But most of all the songs. This woman is a fucking, fucking, fucking *genius*!!" (There was applause here. Partly 'cause I think they were encouraging me to quit while I was ahead.)

"Oh, God, there is so much shitty music out there. They fucking hit you with it, everywhere you go. Everywhere, right? The mall. The drugstore. The grocery store. You just get assaulted with shitty music, like Shania Twain, or Britney Spears, or *Nickelback*. It's like getting a dick shoved in your ear. I'm sorry. Excuse me. But Rosalyn Knight is not like a soldier, she's like a fucking five-star general in the fight against this shitty, plastic, trying-to-kill-you music that they pump out on the radio all the time and play in the mall, the drugstore, the grocery store, making you feel like human garbage. Jesus fuck!

"But Rosalyn is out there, every fucking night, just fucking givin' 'er one thousand percent. Singing her life. Singing *our lives*, the way things really are, with jokes! And the best music, real country music, not genetically modified yee-haw robot *rodeo* like a fucking Walmart flower from a miserable slave factory town in China.

"No, but wait, wait, wait, let me fucking *finish*! And she refuses to quit. She refuses to stop. I'm not saying she's aging, I mean, she's aging beautifully. I love that streak of white you got in your cowlick there, babe. We're all aging, and we're all gonna die, but there's so much *fucking pressure* on us women to fucking *quit*! To quit, and retire, and go back and take care of the fucking children. Am I right, ladies? All the ladies in the house? And Rosalyn refuses to fucking do that. She refuses. She is a fucking hero, and that is what I am trying to say. And for those of us who have taken some shots, and believe me, I'm not speaking metaphorically, I mean taken some *fucking shots to the head*, from my ex, *whom some of you know and still hang with, thank you very much* — LET ME FINISH! What I'm saying is, those of us who have taken some shots, and are stuck with babies, *who we love, don't get me wrong here,* and get made to feel like now that we've hit thirty we're not even supposed to be out here at the bar anymore, what Rosalyn does is carry the fucking flag, and say, 'Hey! Fuck you! Don't tell me what to do. I'm a woman, I'm gonna live my life on my own terms, I'm gonna write awesome songs about that, and I'm not gonna fuckin' back down ! So there!'

"SO LET'S FUCKING PROPOSE A TOAST TO ROSALYN FUCKING KNIGHT, PEOPLE!! WHOOO!!"

And then I drained my beer and demanded another one and then I stage-dove.

There were mixed reviews of the speech. There were. Some people thought it was awesome, and some people thought it was embarrassing. Some people totally blanked me when they saw me downtown after that, and some people, years later, still come up to me and congratulate me on that speech. They say, "I still remember that amazing speech you gave for Rosalyn at her show. I wish I had a tape of that speech; I'd play it for myself every morning as my alarm clock." And it mostly, not entirely, sad to say, breaks down on gender lines, I have to say. Sure, some of the women, especially the younger pretty-little-blond women, were like, "Who the fuck is this bitch? I've never even seen her before. She's not part of the scene. Who does she think she is?" but most of them, all the ones who come up to me even now and remember that speech, it's the chicks, man. The dudes, the dudes never come up to me about that speech. And you could tell that for them it was a showbiz no-no. They just stood there with their arms crossed. I fucking hate dudes with their arms crossed. Brody was cool with it, though, when I checked with him. He was like, "That's punk rock. That's what it's all about, baby. The music moved you, you did what you were moved to do. What more do you want from music, music lover?" And of course Rosalyn was cool with it. Or if she wasn't, she always had the sensitivity not to mention it. I guess she knows I still love her.

So, the speech, the impact of the speech, the speech itself, that was, debatable. I'm not sorry about the speech. The rest of the night things went a little more pear-shaped. I had to make some apology calls about the rest of the night.

I was in the crowd, sort of crowd-surfing. I remember that for sure. I don't remember punching the guy in the face who I had thrown a drink at earlier. Friends who were there didn't see that either. It's more likely that I just semi-accidentally elbowed him as I was going down from the stage-dive. At any rate, apparently he had a "bruised jaw."

Then I did some dancing in the crowd, then I got back up onstage and did some more singing. And I had my arm around DD, who was playing fiddle, and she didn't seem to mind. And then we went offstage with the crowd roaring, and there was this ecstatic feeling as Rosalyn raised her plastic glass to us backstage and said, "Well, we fooled 'em again." And the stomping kept going so we went back on and we sang the finale about meeting our love at the ferry terminal and swayed à la "We Are the World."

Then we partied down on the dance floor to some canned music and it was a beautiful celebration of all Rosalyn's crazed magic, and DD was the centre of it for me, and I was the centre of it for her, and Rosalyn and Brody and the other band people sort of zimmed in and out of our orbit.

Then we got in Saul's cab with some people to Chambers Towers. I remember that because I got in beside Justin, who was in the midst of transitioning. I remember that because I was like, "Shove over, bitch!" in this affectionate way to Justin, but then I realized my mistake so I was like, "Oh, sorry. Shove over, asshole!" but he just told me to go fuck myself.

Do you know that moment? The moment where you know you've gone too far? Where you realize there was a point where you should have stopped consuming alcohol and/or dope, and that that point passed about ten minutes ago? And now all the stuff has been metabolized and suddenly being wasted goes from being a fun party, to being terrible, terrible, terrible? I hate that moment. I remember that moment from that night. We dropped off Justin, who didn't feel like partying with us for some reason that might have been my fault, and then Saul started the cab going again. And I was suddenly, "Oh. Uh-oh. Oh no." You know?

At that moment, where you cascade over the edge, from fun to pain, you have this terrible desire to, you know, go back in time. Go back in time, run to the bar, and knock that drink out of your hand, *stupid idiot.* But you know you can't do that. You know you have bought yourself a ticket on the Spinning Puke Bus. And once you are on the Puke Bus, you are going to have to ride that bus all the way to the station ... and the station basically goes all the way to the evening of the next night, when you will finally have some kind of unbroken human sleep again. You have bought the ticket and there is no way off that bus. There is nothing you can drink, pop, or do that's going to get you off that bus. This terrible, terrible nausea and dizziness and regret and head hurting and sadness is going to stay with you till the end of the line.

I told Saul, "I'm not gonna make it to Rosalyn's. I have to go home," and he nodded. He understood. Saul has been there.

We had to stop three times as Saul piloted me the ten-minute drive to my house, so I could get out and upchuck all over some poor taxpayer's fucking lawn at one thirty in the morning. Somebody, and knowing the City of Victoria, that somebody was some elderly white person, was gonna wake up tomorrow to find half-digested pasta shaped like bunnies, plus bar snacks and beer and tequila and box wine and stomach bile in a big pile on their lawn, killing the grass with its aggressive acidity.

And speaking of old white people, I had a sudden revelation after the third puke stop: "Mother." I know I said it aloud because DD squeezed my hand in sympathy. I said it two more times, in a wailing lament. What I'm saying is I was not looking forward to seeing her, in the state I was in. That's when DD stepped up. And no matter what happened after, the lies, the cheating, the madness, the leaving, the emotional torturing, the leaving again, I will always be grateful for that moment when DD decided to get out of that cab with me and help me get into that house and face that woman who is my mother.

Even as drunk and stoned and just fucking awfully insensate with horror and pain as I was, I could still actually *see* the waves of judgment emanating from my mother, like heat off a blacktop highway in August, through the walls of the house and hitting me in giant bursts of esteem-crushing belittlement. The waves of judgment literally knocked me off my feet as I got out of the cab. DD paid Saul.

DD helped me up the walk and through the door and there she was, silent, glaring, using her obligatory body language. I remember saying, "Don't you realize what a cliché it is to be standing there with your hands on your hips like that?"

She took a deep breath. She was really getting ready to let it rip on me. I was steeling myself for it.

"Hi, Gayle." For a crucial moment, DD interrupted the beam of destructive nasty energy between Mother and me. "I got a hold of those transcriptions for those Bach cantatas I was talking to you about. Do you want me to play a bit of it for you?"

Mom blinked, as if awakened. She looked at DD, as if only now noticing her presence. "You don't think it would disturb the baby?"

DD had taken the fiddle out of her case in a half second and was rosining up already.

"No, I'll play quiet, it's fine. Besides, I used to get babies to sleep in their cribs playing Bach when I was babysitting as a teenager."

I stood as still as if I was in a minefield. DD tuned up quick, played a chord to test, and then started in on the Bach.

My mother didn't say anything. She sat down at the kitchen table. She closed her eyes to listen as the music flowed through the house. The music of comforting, ultra-complex, beautiful order. I don't know a lot about classical music, like DD does, but Bach always makes me feel like maybe there is evidence of a creator mind in the mathematics that holds the universe together. That's how it makes me feel. Like there is reason behind the madness and the shit. Even inside the madness and shit, there's some kind of exquisite math that people just can't normally understand, but it's there and you can understand it if you just listen to Bach and his melodies that bing around like futuristic satellite space explorers, describing the contours of a perfect system.

When my mother closed her eyes, I took the opportunity to sit down on the couch. I still felt like utter slopping-around excrement, but it seemed like if I could just keep my mouth shut and let DD play, I might escape the Mom-o-caust that had been sure as anything imminently heading my way for coming home late and being totally fucking inebriated and irresponsible.

And the Bach did soothe me, too. Both me and my mom were being soothed by the same music at the same time, in the same way.

I don't know how long it lasted, but I'd guess twenty minutes or so. Then it came to its inevitable, perfect end. Mom opened her eyes. She sighed a big sigh, looked DD in the eyes, and said simply, "Thank you." DD looked her right back in the eyes and said, "You're very welcome."

And then Mom picked up her purse, said, "Goodnight, both of you," and she left.

As soon as I heard the car's engine start running out on the street, I exhaled. "Holy shit, DD. You are fucking magic. I love you. Thank you." Then I curled up on the couch and passed out cold.

I woke up the next day and DD had the baby in her arms and they were cleaning the kitchen together. And she just stayed. That's how we became an item for real.

MYKOLA LOYCHUCK

BACK BAR, CAMERON HOUSE, TORONTO, 2016

UM ... THIS MIGHT SOUND STRANGE ... but one of the things I particularly like to do most of all on tours with Rosalyn, perhaps one of my favourite things to do in the world, is ... is to be there before a show, when the bar manager or someone who works for the venue is explaining the rules of the venue to her. Especially the rules around drinking and smoking.

I saw her and DD play the last night of the Sugar Refinery, in their nurses' outfits they'd worn at Rock for Choice. The place was getting closed down 'cause they couldn't pay the fines that No Fun City Vancouver imposed on them for this reason or that reason but mainly because No Fun City. So, it was the last song of the last set ever, and Rosalyn took out a pack of smokes, passed one to DD and DD lit them both. Rosalyn took a big drag and as she exhaled she said, "What are they gonna do? Shut us down?"

Smoking in inappropriate, forbidden places, that's a signature Rosalyn move. And it's not only because she enjoys flouting rules but also because she hates being told what to do. I mean she *really, really, really hates* being told what to do, *ever.* When she and Cole Dixon got together, as an official couple, I knew them both well enough to know it could never work out because they were the two people I knew who hated being told what to do more than anyone. I just thought, *how could there possibly be the usual give-and-take of, what do you call it, long-term couple-hood if both people are* — what word am I trying for here — *both people are allergic to compromise of any kind?*

Who was worse? Hard to say. I don't know. That's hard to measure. When they were together, Rosalyn tried to do what Cole wanted to do more than Cole tried to do what Rosalyn wanted — and it nearly killed her to cope with that.

I'm digressing. I can feel myself digressing. What is the point that I'm making? The point is that when someone was explaining to Rosalyn what was and was not allowed, I would watch the expression on Rosalyn's face and feel this rush of vicarious naughty pleasure, because the look she had was this blank, friendly innocence as she nodded and uh-huh'd at them, saying, "Right. Got it."

Maybe this is true only if you know her, but if you look at her forehead and you look at her ears, you see little tiny movements, little twitches, that tell you she's mapping out her plan for when exactly she's going to break every single rule about smoking and drinking that they are laying out, and how she's going to do it. Those little twitching facial muscles betray that she's already privately, inwardly enjoying those smoking and drinking pleasures, and she's not just *laughing* on the inside — the right word is she is *cackling* on the inside.

Some time after the Grifters went their separate ways and before DD joined the Low Johannahs, Rosalyn and I took DD on a cross-Canada jaunt in a little Hyundai Accent with seats that really jammed into your lower back. DD played in both our sets, or sometimes we all just played together, swapping songs, which is something I only like to do with people like Rosalyn who have songs that I truly admire, because otherwise I feel like I would gnaw my own leg off to get off the stage when it's a bad song.

I'm told that although I try to smile and tap my feet so that people won't know that this bad song I'm listening to is hurting me very deeply, I'm told that people, in fact, can tell that I'm very uncomfortable. I'm not a very good liar. I am very easy to read, I am told.

We were in London, Ontario, at the London Music Club. London is a truly terrible place. The downtown is a ... a classic hollowed-out shell with every second shop window boarded up and a smattering of McDonald'ses, Subways, and cheap vinyl ladies' clothing stores. People hang around the corners, exhausted from meth, begging.

There are two things in London that create the employment for the people there. There's the university, which as far as I can tell is a factory that makes crass young drunk people without a thought in their heads, mostly blond or dyed blond. You only have to take a glance at these kids and you know that they're the boring-middle-class-suburbanites-with-SUVs-and-$3,000-strollers of the future.

The other employer is the insurance industry and we all know that any time something fun is getting shut down it's almost always because of insurance. So, that's London, Ontario. London Life. Everybody from western Canada who plays music hates, hates London, Ontario, because it exemplifies everything we hate about Ontario. Campbell Ouiniette liked to say they call it the "Forest City" because that's what they cut down to make it a city.

The London Music Club is actually a multi-venue complex. There's a small proper concert hall up top for music that really draws people out, like shitty, white Ontario blues players who play "Dust My Broom" and "Kansas City" without ever going to Kansas City, so, when you think about it, they're constantly lying about how they're "goin' to Kansas City," and a little basement bar for the likes of us, unknown people. I think there's an evening supper club space that's part of the building, too, but obviously we would never have been allowed in there.

The beauty of the set-up is that when the popular act is playing upstairs, the *shoomp, shoomp* of the bass drum and the rattle of the enthusiastic applause bleeds into your sparsely attended show in the basement, emphasizing the pathos of your situation as a bottom-feeder. That's the London Music Club, and London in general, going out of its way to make sure you don't forget that most people, the vast, vast majority of people, think you're a loser who doesn't really, ah, merit a lot of listening attention.

The general manager lady was already a bit pissed off with us when she started her memorized talk about the rules, because we were late for sound check. Rosalyn doesn't really do sound check, generally.

Anyway the GM lady started by lecturing us veterans of 150 shows a year for the past decade, lecturing us about the importance of reading the attachment to the contract that clearly states that sound check is always at 3:00 p.m. to avoid disturbing the dinner service. We didn't bother explaining that we would have had to have gotten up at 7:00 a.m. to arrive in London by three because we knew from experience that this lady would likely not have seen a 7:00 a.m. wake-up time as the absurdity we did because she was likely not up drinking until 5:00 a.m.

Then she launched into the smoking and drinking rules, and this is when I really perked up, excited to watch the tiny muscle above Rosalyn's left eyebrow. Some Canadians like to watch hockey and listen to the Tragically Hip, but I don't. The way I express my Canadian identity is by watching and enjoying Rosalyn's left eyebrow.

The lady explained that there was no smoking anywhere inside the building. Smoking was allowed on the fire-escape steps and the load-in steps where ashtrays were provided, but not in front of the club because, even with ashtrays provided, allowing smoking in front of the club led to people throwing their butts in the snow where they became a fermented stew of nastiness that surfaced every spring.

She emphasized that it was all right for staff and musicians to duck out into hidden spaces to smoke, but they could not, were not allowed to, must not *ever* bring alcohol outside for any reason. Ever. Especially not while smoking.

I watched Rosalyn nod along to this. The tips of her ears started to wiggle a bit. I could already see her with the glass of red wine in one hand, the burning Du Maurier in the other, elucidating some bizarre and little-noticed law of the universe as DD chortled away. And I could see that she could already see it, too. I don't think she had decided to go completely all-out quite yet though.

There was a crooner of love songs with a moussed-up quiff and a smoking jacket performing upstairs. He called himself Royal Wood. Rosalyn and DD liked him, but I didn't. I found him insipid, partly maybe because he was better looking than me and he was performing upstairs rather than downstairs. I'd been calling him Morning Wood for so long that I actually slipped up and referred to him as Morning Wood to the face of the GM lady when I asked if he'd be on at the same time as our show (yes, he would). His full band's boobley romantic sounds were sure to waft through our performance, reminding us of our place in the hierarchy.

The lady then handed us our drink tickets. She spelled out that the tickets were for draft beer and well drinks (no labelled liquor from the shelves). Rosalyn smirked. No mention of wine at all. I knew she was at that moment giving herself permission to behave badly, but I couldn't stop myself, I had to wallow in the moment, I had to make sure, so I asked, "And wine? Do the tickets get us house wine?"

She kind of frowned at me and said, "There's no house wine, per se. If you want wine, you have to purchase it at staff discount."

I was thinking *oh boy*, and I just had to go deeper. "What's staff discount?"

She answered that one annoyedly, because anywhere that does things a certain way, where the people who run the place don't travel much, they always act like their rules are the only sensible rules, the only possible rules that could exist. Like when you try to buy beer at a supermarket in Kristiansand, Norway, and it's 8:01 p.m., and the cashier rolls his eyes at you because you're so dumb that you don't know that beer may not be sold in a supermarket after 8:00 p.m. This lady was like that. "Um, ten percent. You know." No, we didn't. So that was it. That was the permission Rosalyn needed to … to aggressively flout authority.

The first time the manager lady came out to the basement steps to remind Rosalyn and DD (and, all right, me, too, I admit it) that alcoholic beverages were not allowed outside, she kept her temper pretty well. It was a simmering tone. We were apologetic. We slapped our foreheads in frustration with our poor memories. It wasn't too bad.

I actually decided not to do it again. I kind of hung in the doorway. I don't smoke, thank God, because I have enough self-sabotaging compulsions. DD either smokes or doesn't smoke, depending on who's around. She appears to have no withdrawal symptoms when she's hanging around with people who don't smoke, but when she's with Rosalyn, she smokes and smokes, and she has nic-fits from not smoking, just like Rosalyn.

I used to believe Rosalyn's pose, her adamant position, that her fanatical pursuit of smoking, drinking, talking, and laughing was merely an indulgence in sheer hedonistic, lazy, selfish time-wasting. Ask her, and she will swear up and down that she is "one of the grasshoppers that played in the sun while the ants stored up nuts for the winter." Don't be deceived. Rosalyn is always working.

I didn't figure it out until a few tours in. Every night on tour, Rosalyn would find some people who were up for the party, and she'd be the last of the touring company of musicians and hangers-on to go to bed. We're talking average between three and six in the morning. Sometimes nine in the morning. Only the Irish in Ireland ever outlasted her, to my knowledge. She would doze in the van or on the train, be bitchy around 5:00 p.m., perk up at dinner, do a fantastic show, and then party onward into another night. Every night. She's made of iron. Party iron. I swear.

I would attempt to keep up with her as best I could, often because I was probably trying to stay up late enough to see if some particular girl there was really interested in making out with me or just liked my music. Inevitably, I would crash out, tired and lonely and blue-balled, and Rosalyn would still be rolling. Telling stories, developing running gags, stumbling across plays on words, and riding her hobby horses about the nature of the music business, the nature of music, the nature of love, the nature of the world.

And every time she'd launch into one of those themes, I'd sigh to myself and think, *There she goes again.* I didn't notice how the themes were mutating, developing. I didn't recognize that the repetition was taking on a more and more definite shape.

I think it was the album *Sauntering Through the Hellfire* that sprung the startling truth on me — the title track and most of the others were made of the hobby horses that Rosalyn had been riding all through those tours of the previous year. The themes and ideas had been cultivated, stacked, and then *fucking rhymed.* The partying of the past year had been this devious, deceptive exercise in songwriting R&D, and I'd been thinking the whole time that we had just been pissing the time away.

The second time the lady came out to tell us off, she wasn't so sweet.

Although I had resolved not to go out there with my beer in hand again, I admit that I was actually out there with my beer in my hand. But I hadn't wanted to.

Stop everything. Wait. I realize that I've been saying bad stuff about London and the London Music Club, and that makes me feel like a total jerk, because I really didn't want to be a jerk to this lady and the London Music Club. I mean, London is ugly, but the people running the London Music Club were actually trying to make London a better cultural place to be, trying to be part of the solution, make life better, support live music when nobody else cares to do that. There was probably some terribly officious Ontario Liquor Board inspector who had failed the actuarial exam at London Life and was putting all the bitterness of his failed insurance career into trying to catch the London Music Club in an Upper Canada Liquors Regime infraction and wanted nothing more than to slap the club with some massive fine so it would go out of business, and I didn't want to be a party to that, of course. No. I am really very much in favour of the London Music Club, even if I'd rather not play there.

But I had real trouble hanging around listening to Royal Wood when I could be on the edge of a parking lot listening to Rosalyn and DD.

By now they had gathered a small crowd of fellow smokers.

"... and then we stayed with those activist kids in Peterborough, right? You know when you meet someone and you just know that their house is gonna smell like cat piss? How is it that one always knows?"

DD belched. "Could be because *they* smelled like cat piss."

"That might be it."

"Yeah, but you went there anyway."

"Well, the pickings were slim. There was that guy with the white cargo van. He was obviously going to murder us with a drill. At least with the vegan activist kids, you know they're so anemic they don't have the strength to kill you. And they can't eat you, 'cause they're vegans, right?"

"One time I went home with this girl who had three cats and, like, fifty different kinds of dildos."

"Fifty? That's too much dildo. That's a dildo glut. That's a flock of dildos. A murder of dildos?"

DD said, "First thing she says to me when we get home is 'how do you identify?'"

And Rosalyn piped in, "Sex-ay!"

They went on and on, bantering back and forth. DD said, "And I'm lying there with like, seventy dildos around my head, and these nine cats are jumping on me, and I can't fucking move."

"Were you tied up?"

"Was I?" Then DD paused, frowning. "No, I was just really drunk."

"Oh. Yes?"

"It was like being tied up, because I wanted to leave, but I couldn't move, and I couldn't really speak. And there's all these dildos."

"What did you tell her about how you identified?"

"I was like, 'Uhhh, me DD.'"

Then the manager lady came out in the middle of the dildo/cat story, and said, "Okay. I've had it. I've now told you *three times* that you can't have alcohol out here. The next time I see you out here, you'll stay out here because you're not coming back in."

DD said, "But we're playing tonight! You have to let us back in or we have to play out here."

The woman looked at DD and said, "People like you are the reason why London's music scene can't get off the ground," and stormed off.

The third time they were heading out, drink in hand, for a smoke, I said, "Hey!" and they turned to look at me.

"Um, you know, if she catches you out there again, we'll probably never be allowed to play here again." They both raised their eyebrows and smiled a little Mona Lisa half smile at me, each doing the identical smile. And Rosalyn's eyebrow said, "Oh, yes?"

This time I really didn't go out there. I just couldn't. I felt like a total wuss for it, but I just couldn't face another confrontation. I stayed inside, drank the beer, listened to Royal Wood, and ate some old Bridge Mix I had in my inner coat pocket.

Ten minutes later, the lady stormed out into the parking lot. She screamed, "Do you people think that the *rules don't apply to you*?!"

There was a silence. DD looked at Rosalyn. Rosalyn looked at DD. A knowing look. Then the laughter, which went on until 4:00 a.m.

Fourteen months later, UnMatched Records released the new full-length Rosalyn Knight album, a chronicle of a delirious love affair gone south, entitled *The Rules Do Not Apply to Us*.

AMY WILLIAMS

HER KITCHEN, FERNWOOD NEIGHBOURHOOD, VICTORIA, 2014

WE WERE ABSOLUTELY BROKE. I owed my mother twelve hundred bucks, which she knew was never going to be paid back. And there was always a danger with her that if I asked for too much help, she'd try to take the baby from me. We were living on food DD got Dumpster diving. She could pick the lock on the containers outside Overwaitea Foods. Mostly bread and cheese a day past their due date. Rent was due in a week. DD had just come back from tour, and they had earned seventy bucks each. DD called Brody to see if there was any roofing work to be had, but the weather had been lousy and nobody was calling him. He was at home by the phone with his thumb up his ass, watching *The World at War* documentary series again.

Our lives together in the past had been one romantic transgression after another. We had been each other's guilty pleasure, we had been each other's break from reality. Now we were completely ensnared in reality. I'd like to say we knew that as long as we had each other, we'd be okay, but in fact it felt like shit. I felt ugly and stupid and lame, having been left behind on the tour once again, but this time by DD, and here she was, back at home, and I was The Wife, demanding to know what the fuck we were gonna do about the looming first of the month. But I really needed to know. You know?

That's when she started going through my clothes and picking out the femmiest ones. Shit she would never wear in a million years. She'd let her hair grow while on tour, a sure sign she was feeling low. She started to brush it out in front of the mirror, while pawing through my makeup bag.

"What the fuck are you doing with my stuff? Something's going on here."

She turned to face me, full-on, eye-to-eye. "Got any hairpins?"

"What's going on?"

"I'm getting dressed up. Gonna go see some friends of mine."

The realization dawned on me, about what she was doing, but I didn't want it to be true so I pretended that it hadn't dawned on me. I knew what kind of work she'd done when she lived in Quebec. She had some funny stories about some of the odd kinks that dudes had, like rubber dresses, diapers, other stuff they couldn't get their wives to do for them. But that was years ago. It gave her an edge that she'd been tough enough to do that kind of work, but that was years ago. It was in the past. It wasn't what was happening *now*, just because somehow we'd run out of options. No way.

"What friends?"

"Old friends from before I met you. They're going to help us out. I'm taking the car for a bit."

"You can't have the car. We need it to do some errands. He needs to get his shots."

She looked at me again. "Okay. You can drop me off."

I wonder how straight, regular people square their idea that the cops are there to uphold the law and protect people, with the fact that everybody knew for decades where the Hells Angels' Esquimalt clubhouse was. Like, what explanation do they give themselves that it's common knowledge where these guys operate out of, and that that place never changes? Maybe they think it's liberal judges or something, protecting these guys' "rights" from cops who really do want to arrest them but just can't? I don't know.

I was running that over in my mind, wishing I could call the cops and stop this thing from happening, as we pulled up to the curb. You really wouldn't have recognized her, all dolled up, as it were. She was a very pretty girl.

"You don't have to do this."

"Gotta go to work, baby. We need the money. It's just work."

"We can find another way to pay the rent. Please don't."

She stepped out of the car, gave me a kiss on the cheek, and leaned in to kiss Wyatt.

"Don't wait up for me. I'll be back late."

MYKOLA LOYCHUCK

BACK BAR, CAMERON HOUSE, TORONTO, 2016

I NEVER UNDERSTOOD WHY, I mean I always felt it was a … a mistake for DD to join the Johannahs. I didn't see the *why* of it. I didn't think it was a good thing for DD, or necessary. It was just a bad fit. On the face of it maybe it seemed like a good fit. But it wasn't.

I tend to think a lot about things, and sometimes people tell me I think too much, so I really have thought about whether the reason I thought DD joining the Johannahs was a mistake was because I wanted DD to keep playing with me. I really think that, although, yes, I felt jealous of their success, and yes, I was angry that in Kris's own words (said in a "ha ha, joking with you!" kind of way) they "stole" DD from me after seeing us play together, even so, I think DD joining the Low J's was a bad idea for DD's sake, and not merely for my own. Maybe I'm not qualified to say that but that's what I think.

I was part of a workshop with the Johannahs and this terrible band called Fruit at the Vancouver Folk Festival — you know what a workshop is. Oh, okay. For anyone reading who doesn't know … in my own words … um … it's something that only happens at Canadian folk festivals. Everybody, say, three or four different groups or solo acts, they get put up on the same stage at the same time and each act takes a turn doing a song, and if you want you can all jam on it. Or not. It can be magic, or it can be a real dog's breakfast. The artistic director will give the thing a cute name in the program, like "Grrrrls with guitars" or "Home Songs from Distant Shores" or some other nonsense.

So, it was me with DD on accompaniment, the Low Johannahs, and Fruit. The title of this workshop was something like "Transgression Airways" or whatever. Because I sing about left-wing politics sometimes and I had DD in my band and Fruit were lesbians and the Low Johannahs sang about dark things and were women, I guess.

Fruit were not terrible because they were lesbians, of course, and they were not terrible because they were Australians, as Cam would try to tell you. They were terrible because they were terrible. There is so much terrible music out there. And Fruit were just part of the vast ocean of terrible music, music that gets made by people who are out there on the make, trying to use music to get something, to get somewhere, or something.

For instance, they did a cover of "Walk on the Wild Side" by Lou Reed. This is a terrible idea, right off, because Lou Reed generally disavowed "Walk on the Wild Side" — it had been overplayed and he felt it was overproduced, and he knew that people generally liked it for the wrong reasons. It was his biggest hit. That's kind of terrible right there, choosing someone's most popular song as the one you're going to cover, which you can only do if you're going to do something really different with it. But Fruit did not. They did it kind of note-for-note, except they exteeended it, and made the saxophone solo looonger and fake-orgasmic squeal-skwonking at the end, and they changed the famous lead-in to the chorus. Where Reed says, "And the coloured girls go doo-de-doo, de-doo, doo-de-doo-doo," they changed *coloured girls go* to *everybody sing* because it's racist to say *coloured girls* as an anachronistic way to evoke a bygone era of female backup singers in sequins and chiffon.

I suppose it probably is racist, but if you think a songwriter is racist for saying *coloured girls* then it is my personal opinion that maybe you should just pick somebody else's song to cover?

The Low Johannahs were in a particularly low moment of their um, band dynamic at that point. Desiree had left the band, and the other three were fighting like sisters of the same abusive home.

The thing about them was that although they could all be absolutely awful to each other, in general they had very good taste. They were visibly squirming through "Walk on the Wild Side," as was I, I was told later. I thought I was smiling along, showing that I was part of the camaraderie, but I was told later that I wasn't. So, I was not contributing. I was accidentally sabotaging the vibe, again. [Sighs.]

Still, I had DD with me. She had already played on one of my songs earlier in the workshop, and so the Fruit women were already zeroed in on her. When the giant sax solo came up — I should mention that it was a Kenny G–style soprano saxophone, which is less like a saxophone and more like a pathetic, tinny clarinet, and all soprano saxophones should probably be melted down into blobs of gilded metal and buried with all the waste from used plutonium deep under a mountain in Arizona and never be played by anyone — anyway, the saxophone player turned to DD and said, "Come on, let's go!" as if they were going to have this amazing collaboration onstage.

DD was game in those days. She hadn't played a lot on those kinds of stages, and she is a very open person, so she really gave it her best shot. But the sax player was only pretending to be collaborating on a thing with DD. At first DD tried to respond, improvisationally, to what the sax player was playing. But the sax player was not, in fact, improvising. The sax player was playing a solo that had been written, a solo that surely was played the same way every time Fruit covered that dumb song. The solo had a *path* it was going on, and that path was leading inexorably to a series of the kind of sonic fake orgasms that really please crowds of people who don't know how easy that is to just jizz a bunch of accelerating notes all over the stage. The solo ended with the sax player *on her knees*, saxing it up in front of DD, making eye contact without making any real contact. It was a kind of attack.

The song took a long time to be over. Fruit had eaten up about fifteen minutes of stage time with their extended Lou Reed cover. I've been told that I was chewing my arm at the end.

When it was finally over, it was the Low Johannahs' turn. Suzie leaned into the mic and said, "Wow … that was a real walk on the wild side." Deadpan. Then she said, "This is a Townes Van Zandt song called 'Tecumseh Valley.'" It was a good moment. I think … I think, looking back on it, it was important to the Low Johannahs how much it was like a Low Johannahs moment from the early days of their band. I knew they'd win DD over with it. And they did. She knew pretty much every Townes song, and this one about a country girl who falls into prostitution and dies alone and diseased, that was Low Johannahs territory, all right. She knew they were going to nod her way after the second chorus, and when they did she dropped a … a *motherfucker* of a minimal solo. Just really one note, buzzing away like a chainsaw, conveying the whole J's vibe of determinedly morose bloody-minded woman-ness.

The solo sounded like an abortion in an alley or something. It was a total rebuke to the extended "Walk on the Wild Side." Fruit just sat there, not even trying to jump in on it. They knew.

That's how the Low Johannahs got hooked on DD, and they used the lure of the money and the big tours and venues to hook her into their deal, away from me.

LILA AUSTIN

VIDEO SHOOT, SAN FRANCISCO, 2015

THE LOW JOHANNAHS. THOSE BITCHES. I am sooo glad to be out of that band. If I had to sing "Hummingbird Café" one more time, I swear to fucking God I'd blow my goddamn brains out, I shit you not. I am so glad to be the boss lady of my own project. I decide what I sing, I decide what I record. I don't have to check in with no fuckin' committee of no fucking crazy fucking perpetually-on-the-rag crazy fucking bitches any more. Jesus.

DD wasn't ever really fully in the band, exactly. She was, like, our effort to save things when they were at their most craziest.

The second record had just come out and nooobody was happy with it. Kris had just pulled her shit-fit at the Chicago listening party, where they had sushi because the album was called *Oppenheimer Park*, which is in the middle of old Japantown in Vancouver, although it's mostly junkies there now.

Anyway, Kris had started screaming because she had decided that she had a violent allergy to MSG, and when she said her allergy was violent she meant she was gonna *do* some fuckin' violence because bitch didn't want no fuckin' sushi! I'm telling you. It was crazy. She fuckin' flung that raw fish around, it was whappin' into the gathered members of the press, the U.S. booking agent, Marc, and all the execs at Moevment Music. What a shitstorm of raw fish. There *was* no MSG in there. But Kris would just fly into these fuckin' *rages* over who-the-fuck-knows-what. Suzie was worse; she would sulk. I've never seen anybody sulk like Suzie could sulk. She could have sulked for the U.S. Olympic Sulking Team.

This was when me and Patrick were in the middle of this bitter fucking breakup and custody battle over Zeb, and Patrick was using the fact that I was a *musician* as an argument against me having custody of *my kid* because everybody knows that musicians, especially female musicians, are loose-vagina'd, alcoholic drug fiends who have no sense of responsibility ... conveniently forgetting here that Patrick was fucking *desperate* to be a musician himself, and made demos that I, in my foolishness, even passed along to Marc and some other record companies. But no, since I had *realized* the dream that he had *failed* at, I was an unreliable parent, if you can fucking believe that.

So I was a little on edge, too, at the time, I admit. But those bitches were not helping. No, they were not. I am *so glad* I don't have to see their ugly bitch faces every day. I'd blow my brains out. Hand me the gun. I am not joking.

I guess when I think about it, we were all pretty fucked up about a lot of stuff. I had my deal, my damage or whatever, my rebellious past ... I ran away from home at thirteen and hung out with some bad people; I didn't talk to my mom for six or seven years. And Kris, there, was raised by a chemical-weapons scientist guy and his ex-missionary wife who was an undiagnosed paranoid schizophrenic and would put nacho chips in a bowl of iced tea and tell the kids to eat their Mexican soup. And Suzie was black but adopted by racist white people. I guess we had a lot of shit going on.

That's the environment we brought DD into, so I guess it isn't that hard to see why she ran away from it. I guess the mystery is *where* she ran and why she won't tell nobody where she ran. And the other mystery is why she stayed in that shitstorm so long. And the other mystery is why I stayed in it so long. I'd rather blow my fucking brains out with a goddamn .45 Magnum than go back to that.

AMY WILLIAMS

HER KITCHEN, FERNWOOD NEIGHBOURHOOD, VICTORIA, 2016

I KNEW SHE WAS ALREADY FUCKING AROUND on the road, just from the fact that her phone calls started to get less frequent and shorter and she kept trying to end them with the word *anyways*.... I knew that there was somebody she was probably seeing in Vancouver, just on account of how she always said she hated the "Big Smoke" and suddenly she was there a lot for one reason or another.

Mainly, there was just a tone ... I'd say I was missing her or complain about something that was bugging me and she'd just kind of widen her eyes as if to say, "what do you want me to do about it?" It made me realize *I* had become the crazy, controlling bitch in her life. When I tried to confront her about it, and point out the specific little things she was doing that she used to do to the girls she was cheating on with me, she would suddenly have things she definitely urgently needed to get done outside the house, and work needed to get done, you know? She had this way of looking at you, wounded, when you caught her in a lie, as if *you* had failed *her* somehow by pointing it out.

Although it did surprise me when she and Miruna moved together to Galiano, because I thought DD was done with that island. But I also knew I shouldn't be surprised, since the smaller the island, the easier it was for her to trap her hostage on it while she went back on the road. And morally I really had no leg to stand on, since, like I told you before, I played a role in breaking up a few relationships she'd been in over the previous decade. I sure as hell played a role in what Rosalyn called "DD's trail of crying ladies" before I became one of them, and I admit that I still cherish the memory of some of those episodes (and when I say *cherish*, of course, I mean *jerk off to*). I'll never forget when I busted her and Jasmine up, which I'm still not sorry about, when I knew Jasmine was out of town and I went over in those fuck-me boots and the short private-schoolgirl skirt. Did I tell you about this already? Yeah, I guess I like telling this story. Ha. No, yeah, I'm sure it was Jasmine she was with then. I had just started seeing Jacob at the time.

She looked at me when she opened the door, and just gulped and said, "Oh, dear." — I know I told it before. I'm gonna tell it again, goddamn it, and you're gonna listen. — As soon as she let me in, I could see the boots were working on her so I just writhed around on the hardwood floor on my hands and knees, saying things like, "I just really need you to fuck me right now. It doesn't have to *mean* anything." And that pretty much worked. DD was almost never without a steady girl that I ever knew of. Okay, actually, *never* never. She just swung between girls like Tarzan from vine to vine. There was never any real gap between letting one girl go and grabbing another. So, in the case of Jasmine I just really poisoned that relationship so that I'd be the next available vine; I have to admit to myself that's what I did. I actually turned out to be a few more vines away, but she got to me eventually. I would feel worse about it if, for one thing, I didn't just fucking hate Jasmine, and still do — no, I have *contempt* for her. Contempt. But also because it was eventually done to me, and deep down I probably knew it was going to happen but I was just on this trajectory by that point. Like a shot arrow. I couldn't deviate from my DD path.

Yeah, so, in that case, I was the home wrecker, so to speak, and so I guess I had it coming when my home got wrecked by Miruna (although I don't blame Miruna, I blame DD). I was the home wrecker in the fuck-me boots, but in reality, in my internal reality, I was just giving up. I was just going over there in those fuck-me boots like a zombie, with no moral agency of my own, just like an iron filing flying at an electric magnet. I was just like, "What's the use of resisting? It's gonna happen sooner or later." Because, like I said, it's no exaggeration to say that we broke up at least five long-term relationships because I wound up getting loaded and fucking DD again, and then the repercussions would come.

Sometimes I wonder, was she just my excuse? Was she just my safety valve, my escape hatch when things got stale with some lover that I'd made the mistake of making all those stupid promises to, the ones you make when you think you're deep in the *love* and I guess all that natural OxyContin or whatever is coursing through your veins? But no. The problem was that throughout my twenties I was like a compass needle, and no matter what other magnets would draw me, or make me spin around or whatever, I would always find myself pointing at her. So, that's why the fuck-me boots and all the other times after that — I just figured, fuck *it*, you know? Because I'd tried resisting, I'd tried being good. I obviously just couldn't do it. I wasn't strong enough. I just had to play it out to its logical conclusion, all the way, and that's what I did. And Jesus Christ what a lot of heartache it brought me. Then again, what a lot of heartache I'd already had from just being around her, and in the end, in the long run, after years and years, it settled the question. I'm *not* supposed to spend my life with her. She is *not* the droids I'm looking for. We just weren't good for each other. Maybe we were too much alike. Although she got to do a lot more with her music than I did, probably mostly because I got myself knocked up. Don't get me wrong, I love Wyatt more than anyone can love anything; he's the greatest thing that ever happened to me. But DD got to live that dream and go to Europe with Mykola and Romania with you and play all those festivals and hang out with Jimmy Kinnock and be in the Low Johannahs ... and I didn't, because I was home with the kid.

And that's probably what broke us up in the end. She'd be calling from these exotic locations, Belfast, Budapest, Austin, Oakland, Montreal, and I could *hear* the party going on, and the music I wasn't hip to, and the glasses clinking and breaking, and the stupid horny laughter of extremely drunk young women. When she'd sign off her phone call with, "Anyways … love you! Talk tomorrow," it would literally grind me, just grind my guts with envy and resentment for not being allowed to go to the party.

I don't think it was the *fact* that I *knew* there were women out there, and she was sleeping with them, and looking in their eyes all googly, and brushing their bangs out of their eyes with gentle care like she used to do with me. Although I was pretty choked about that, and about how insulting the perfunctory, unconvincing denials were. She's such a liar. But I think, more than anything, what I felt shitty about was that I wanted to be there *too.* Well, fuck. That's life, I guess. Anyway, it was probably never as fun as it sounded on the other end of the phone from two continents away.

Eventually, and it was a long, hard road, I got her out of my system. She worked her way through me, wrecking everything in my system as she went. But she is out of me now. I have a great thing going with a genuinely honest, *good* person, through and through. And being good does *not* mean being boring, after all, dammit.

I mean, if, one day, we were both old, and retired, and we'd both mellowed a lot with time, I can sort of imagine us being real friends again, maybe living in the same neighbourhood, visiting each other for tea like nice old ladies. And I still have the boots.

MIRUNA MOLNAR

FERRY FROM GALIANO ISLAND TO VICTORIA, 2016

WAS SHE A HIPPY? I DON'T KNOW. What is a hippy? Am I a hippy because I make kombucha and I have long hair and I like to live outside the city, as sustainably as I can? Yes, she did smoke a lot of weed. Well, mostly little bits of weed, or hash in that little pipe of hers, all day.

Yes, we kept our own chickens. We used to argue about who was going to get up in the morning in the freezing cold and let the chickens out of their coop. She was the one who talked me into getting them, and named them all. So I thought she should be the one to deal with them and clean the chicken house, especially since I dealt with them all the time when she was on tour. Including when a raccoon got in with them and left the most brutal bloody mess, like a serial-killer crime scene. I threw up in the chicken yard when I saw it, and then I threw up again when I went back to try to confront it and smelled my own vomit. Gross, gross, gross!

Yes, we had goats for a while. We sold the goats. Our lady goat, Belinda, had kids, and DD named the male kid "Tom-Tom" because she was already planning to kill him, skin him, and make a drum out of him. He was super affectionate. He would just nuzzle up to you, warm and fuzzy like a living stuffed animal. But boy goats get really aggressive when they hit puberty. They start getting very smelly and butting everything and everyone right in the crotch. Yes, she chopped his head off with an axe. It was really quick, but I couldn't eat him, although I know I've eaten goat before lots of times at Ethiopian and Jamaican restaurants — but I couldn't eat him. I would've puked him up again. I couldn't go through that again, so we sold the other goats. But yes, she nursed him with a bottle, she raised him, and she chopped his head off with an axe. Is that a hippy thing to do?

It was right around that time that she started getting a lot of postcards from Rosalyn Knight, from the road. "Hi from your old stomping grounds in Belfast," "Greetings from L.A. (Lethbridge, Alberta), miss having you ride shotgun!" that kind of thing. I started to get a little disquieted by that, but she told me I was being silly. I don't believe that I was being silly, in retrospect.

ANONYMOUS

REJECTED REVIEW OF *FERRY LIGHTS* BY THE LOW JOHANNAHS, SUBMITTED TO *BC MUSICIAN MAGAZINE*, 2012 (POSTMARKED MACEDONIA)

THE FACT IS THAT THE LOW JOHANNAHS have been finished now for at least five years. Like the Rolling Stones, or, more locally, Blue Rodeo, the band is a zombie corpse of its former self, cursed to wander the world and make everybody sad for the loss of something magical that can no longer be.

Somebody should take a hatchet to this band, who once created so many perfect moments of inspired misery but are now just going through the motions, miserably. And if you don't know the difference then you'll never know and I can't tell you. The originals are uninspired, and the covers feel phoned in. This reviewer had it from several sources that none of the Low Johannahs were ever even in the studio at the same time for this record. They just individually recorded their tracks, alone, and then mixed them together in post-production. They studio-usly avoided each other.

There are only two bright spots on the whole record. One is a stunning cover of "Tecumseh Valley" by the one and only Townes Van Zandt. The only proof that they didn't record it long ago when they were still playing together like a *real band* is the perfectly woven-in violin part by newcomer DD, formerly of the tragically overlooked Supersonic Grifters, who is largely wasted on the material here. In fact, the only other bright spot is a deceptively simple number penned by DD herself, entitled "You Are Home to Me," which should have been the single, and if they still had competent management like they did in the past, this reviewer is relatively sure that DD would have been asked to contribute more to this pathetic effort, which should otherwise be taken out behind the barn and shot.

2/10.

MYKOLA LOYCHUCK

BACK BAR, CAMERON HOUSE, TORONTO, 2016

HERE'S SOMETHING THAT REALLY GETS ME DOWN sometimes these days … now that I sometimes hang out with really successful musicians, people … people who play to theatres full of adoring fans who know all their songs or at least the hits. The thing is, it's quite striking how many of them are … miserable. Cole Dixon has struggled with what you could definitely call, what I would say, in my professional opinion, is clinical depression. Several of the lady-singers I've met had severe eating disorders, scarfing down pizza and then throwing it up in the alley behind the bar. It's a little bit of a mess out there. The whole idea is to work your way to living your dreams … but a lot of the dream-livers are having such a terrible time that the dream is starting to threaten my interior life, like the dream is partly a light that's moving farther and farther away, but also a looming monster that I've seen eat people.

I know, I mean, I always knew that was a thing that rock stars talked about in their songs and in interviews, but in the past I imagine I was ignoring that sort of thing, dismissing it as pampered whining. Now I'm not quite as sure that I should dismiss it. I'm not sure what the route to happiness might be, but what I'm saying is that this route that I had unconsciously — or maybe … maybe it's more accurate to say *consciously* — planned for myself is looking sort of like a dead end if I look at it too hard. So I don't look at it too hard most of the time. That's my strategy.

The Low Johannahs were the first musicians I knew personally who went from unknowns to stars. From being dirty tree-planter girls swapping Mississippi John Hurt songs by the campfire, to going on Letterman and headlining festivals and having herbal tea at Emmylou Harris's house. And they seemed to be having a terrible time.

I think the real idea behind taking DD into the band was to find some antidote to the misery. Hoping that DD might help them find a path back to … to the joy of making music together. She clearly had a door that opened in that direction. Individually, each of the Johannahs was capable of going there with her, but as a group, it just wasn't happening. Or, not often enough to make it work, and my personal theory is that their misery is what drove her underground.

The one thing I loved about them when they were at their worst was the stage banter. Punk rockers are supposed to not give a fuck what people think, but those women, they *really* did not. Did not care. I would say that there are unwritten rules about things you're never supposed to say from the stage. I would say that they seemed to have a checklist of them, and they would sometimes seem to be running down the list, doing all the things you don't do.

It's important to be in tune. "I tune because I care," that's what Rosalyn always says. That's true. But one of them or the other would each choose a space between a different song to tune up their instrument, and of course they couldn't begin a song while one of them was tuning. There would be these amazing epochs, eons of dead air in their sets, where they'd just be going *twing … twing … twing.*

And then … one of them would take it upon themselves to fill that awkward time and speak. And that would be worse than dead air. All to a vast sea of, say, five to ten thousand paying people in a festival mainstage crowd.

One time, I think it was the fest in Comox, Kris said, "Um, how many of you out there are camping at this fest?" and the crowd cheered, and she said, "That's awesome. So cool that you're camping."

And then Suzie turned to Kris but said into the microphone, "Are you camping?"

And Kris was like, "Um, no."

And Suzie went, "No, you're not, you're staying at the four-star hotel you demanded to be on the rider."

And this was right on the mainstage.

And Kris said, "Well, are *you* camping?"

"Hell no. I hate camping. I'm just saying so do you."

"I camp. I camp sometimes."

"I've never, ever seen you camp."

And Lila finally broke in and said, irritably, "Anyway, let's start the song. You ready? You *tuned* yet?"

And, of course, then Suzie was there with, "Almost. Just gotta get this pesky D string up...."

Twing, twing.

I mean, really. Some of us aspiring performers were just killing ourselves to try to craft entertaining jokes or entertaining introductions to songs, or just trying to find some way to reach out to the audience to get them to, you know, *care* about the song we were about to play, about what we were doing, in the hopes that one day we might break through the giant wall of indifference. And these women were just wasting time, or worse, slagging off their own band members from the stage, and the audience just hung on every word. And when the song *did* start, the crowd went bananas because they recognized the opening four notes of the song from the beloved album. Suzie would introduce a song like this:

"I've been going to Curves lately."

And Lila would go, "What's Curves?"

"It's a place for fat ladies to work out. Fat ladies like me."

"Huh. That's great."

And Suzie would go, "Anyway, I think my arms are getting pretty strong. Let's play 'John Henry.'"

And that was the introduction. Yes, it was.

Sometimes they'd get a bit more on point with the actual subject matter of the song, and sometimes that would, in fact, be even more horrific than the other way.

There was one time I was there watching them from the crowd when Lila said, "Some of you already know this, but in the American folk music tradition, there's a whole bunch of songs where you know, a dude sleeps with some chick."

Suzie: "Some chick?"

Lila: "Sorry, chick is bad, right?"

Suzie: "Yeah. Can't say chick anymore. That's sexist."

Lila: "Some chickie-baby, he sleeps with her, he knocks her up. Puts a bun in her oven. She's 'in the family way.' Then the pressure is on to get married. So, he's thinking about that. But he don't really wanna get married. He's not quite ready to settle down."

Suzie: "He's unsure."

Lila: "He's unsure. He's unsure. So, instead he just kills her. Stabs her with a knife, or drowns her in the river usually. Or both! Then they hang him. I like to call these songs 'Appalachian abortion songs.' And this here is one of 'em."

Speaking of abortion, let's not forget the time I saw them perform at Rock for Choice. Their song selection for the event? An old trad chestnut called "I Wish My Baby Had Been Born." Yes.

There was also the charming habit of apologizing for the sloppiness of the previous song — "Sorry, guys. We'll do that one better next time. I knew we should have run through that in sound check." Or the classic game they played where they each took a turn between songs to ask the monitor guy to turn their own instrument up. "Can I get some more ukulele in the monitor, please," says the ukulele player, followed by, "We could use a little more guitar in the monitor, if you can," from the guitar player. And then ...

"Can I get a bit more vocal here in the monitor?"

"Yeah, me too."

"Mine as well."

Until everything has essentially been made louder than everything else, and so nothing has happened at all, because the mix is a *mix*, of course, and you can't ... oh, never mind. It was a garbage palace that DD walked into. A shipwrecked train.

KRIS HAUSER

CAFE DEUX SOLEILS, COMMERCIAL DRIVE, VANCOUVER, 2014

WE WANTED SOMEONE TO FILL OUT the sound after Suzie left in a huff. And it had to be a girl. That's the deal. You can say, "Oh, that's, you know, discrimination, because you wouldn't leave it open in terms of gender." I find that risible, given the long history of patriarchy in the so-called music business. There are no women musicians out there. There are no jobs for them, no spots for them at festivals. Yes, of course, there's, like, a smattering of female musicians, and it's always the singer — if it's not the singer it's always somehow a big deal. A man is the bass player. A woman is "the girl bass player." You know. And there were issues of marketing. The Low Johannahs had a vibe of, you know, the lady-hobo thing. Boxcar Bertha. Poor, free, adventuring girls on the road. And G totally fit that vibe. I mean, she was *in* a band with DD before.

We needed a female, and I have a general rule: if some girl leaves the band, you replace her by chunking in a lesbian, you know? They're just lower maintenance than straight girls. And I say that as a straight girl. But I'm sorry, it's true. It's true! They spend less time in the bathroom, they're ready to get going sooner, and, most importantly, they don't tend to get accidentally impregnated, generally, so you don't have to chunk in another girl so soon.

But when DD heard that we were going to get G to sit in on a practice, she took me aside, and she looked me in the eye, and she said, "I'm only going to ask this once. If you're my friend, please don't hire G to be in the band."

And I was like, "Okay ... Why? She's cool," and DD was like, "I don't wanna go into that. If you trust me, and you're my friend, just go with me on this one, since I've never asked for anything like that before." So I said, "Okay, copacetic. I'll tell the girls."

But then the others were like, "Why?" and I was like, "DD says no," but they were like, "Yeah, but why?" and I was like, "She won't say," and they were like, "Well, there has to be, like, some kind of *reason* to discriminate against G like that. That's not right," and I was like, "Okay, whatever. I tried."

I explained to DD, and she said, "So, you're taking her in the band anyway?" and I was like "Dude, I tried." She just started picking at her fiddle case. She didn't say anything. So I just assumed it was settled. There were a thousand urgent things to do to get ready for the next round of recording and touring. We couldn't afford to spend a lot of time discussing any one thing. You know?

TOM ABBOTT

KINGSTON'S SECOND OLDEST BAR, AFTER CLOSING, 2015

I SAW DD WHEN SHE CAME THROUGH with Mykola a while back. I made a point of getting out to the Black Sheep to see the show. It was a fuckin' killer. Hosting the open mic, there's sometimes a long lull between nuggets of truly great stuff. You gotta have stamina, you gotta have faith, heh, that the next true moment will come along. But Mykola and DD were just stringing those moments together like a fuckin' pearl necklace that night. Place was half-full, but we all felt privileged to be there.

I'd seen them play before and I liked their thing. Mykola passes off to DD a lot more than most singer-songwriters do with their soloists. He tries to put her in charge of the song, but she only takes charge of it when she feels like it, when she's moved to. So when it fucks up with them, it's because he's asking her to take the reins but she's not there yet, and there can be a second where he loses the thread. Also, when she really takes it he can get so into her playing that you can see he's forgot where the fuck he is in the song. Those mistakes were still there, for sure, but not very many. They were tight-connected by a single attitude that night.

It was kinda like they had found a new gear, and the new gear was quiet. Quietness. They had their usual interaction between

Mykola's voice and DD's fiddle, where he would sing a thing and then she would comment on that and he would change how he sang the next line based on what she just played. I could hear that. I could hear that weird conversation they have up there onstage. That's what I came for. That and all the good songs, built with care like old-fashioned furniture so they have this fuckin' ... solidity to their construction. There were genuine old trad songs in the setlist but Mykola can put together new songs that have the same durable feel as an old song so you can't always tell the difference. I like that.

You sort of half-noticed DD dropping down the dynamics so she'd get quieter and quieter, and Mykola was tuned into that and he'd follow her into the quietness. They would have these moments where they would drop down to just a cunt hair short of silence, and the audience would get sucked right in there till things were freakily still and some duffer in the middle of the crowd would get too nerved out by it and have to cough, but even that didn't ruin it because they stayed quiet in defiance of any background noise. They had this aggressive, punk-rock fuckin' *quiet* going on. Really made me think *I fuckin' need to steal that.* I mean, I know how to do that, but I had kind of half-forgotten. Plus, when they wanted people up on their feet, they were totally able to rock the dance floor, just the two of them. That's super hard to do without a rhythm section.

The Sheep used to be a hotel so there's rooms upstairs. Paul, the owner and Svengali of the place, doesn't really like people going up to the rooms anymore. But the show was so good he kind of relaxed and let us party up there above the bar. If you knew Paul you'd know that meant it was a fucking sick show. DD and I jammed on some of our old tunes. I didn't know then that she was ill, but looking back on it she was pretty pale. Her forehead was a little pinched. She had a little wood pipe and she was leaning out the window and taking hits off little hash chunks pretty regularly, pretty often.

We were all drinking beers, and I told the story I told you about DD getting me back to play the Hullaballoo with her. I said to her, you know, that I'm really grateful to her for setting me on that path, that I really felt that I was in the process of healing after having been such a piece of shit in a lot of ways back then.

DD took a hit off the pipe and really locked eyes with me, the way she used to do in the old days. When DD decides to lock eyes with you, it's this powerful thing. She lets you into this other part of her, and that part of her is kind of a different DD. I don't know. Full of feelings. Pity for the world, deep sadness, anger, and this weird spark of black humour, kind of ironic. Right then I realized that it had actually been, fuck, years, ages since she had done that with me.

She locks eyes with me and says, "That's great. Tom. Good for you. *Good for you.*"

GIULIETTA CAETANO

HER HOUSE, TUCSON, ARIZONA, 2016

OKAY, WITH THE JOHANNAHS. We live in a capitalist society. We all have neo-liberalism up our asses. We have to eat. I was broke, and it was a job. I needed the work, it paid well, and I'm not trying to hide anything, all right? Being in a famous band was a way to get further with my own music, down the road. I kinda had to take the offer. It might have kind of added insult to injury for DD, I see that, but what choice did I have, man?

I know she wasn't cool with it. But it had been several years by then, since the episode. Like I said, I'm not proud of it. If I'd had something else anywhere near as good, I wouldn't have taken the gig, knowing it made her uncomfortable. Seriously, at that time there really were no other opportunities coming my way. I was broke, I was back in the States getting older with no health insurance, and I was out of options.

I tried to give her space on tour. I tried not to crowd her. I stayed on the opposite side of the stage. I was polite, but not fakey-fakey. I knew she didn't want me there. She made that *very* clear to me.

The Johannahs were touring like maniacs then. Striking while the iron was hot. It was surprising how little money we made, given the big crowds, the album sales, the merch. I don't know what was going on there with Moevment. Something creepy.

I was even supportive when DD asked that Rosalyn come on tour with us as an opener, which was a total disaster.

Some people find Rosalyn funny, but like, I'm sorry, I just don't get it. Sad to say, our audience didn't get her either. It was, sorry to say this, a little bit pathetic, this woman pushing forty, all dolled up in her vintage *Hee Haw* dresses, and she would make these weird jokes between songs, like, "Why did Hitler never drink whisky? 'Cause it made him mean," and the audience would just be silent as the grave, man.

DD said it was because our audience was "a bunch of fuddy-duddy, middle-aged, CBC-listening losers with beards and Cowichan sweaters with no sense of humour," but I think there was an edge of desperation to Rosalyn's humour at that point. Frankly, telling the audience at the end of your set to "be sure to have a few drinks to relax behind the wheel on the way home," just isn't super funny, to me. But hey, that's just me.

Then we did another big world tour behind the new record, and it was during that tour that DD started to complain about the pain under her arms.

She got this shocking diagnosis when we got home, and what really blew me away was that instead of staying home to deal with it, she chose to go on tour again — but not with us, with Mykola again, where she knew she'd be playing to, like, as few as ten people a night in some places. Like what's the point in killing yourself like that, when you're already dying?

MYKOLA LOYCHUCK

BACK BAR, CAMERON HOUSE, TORONTO, 2016

WELL, THAT WAS ... WAS A STRANGE TIME, when DD had the lumps under her arm. She had these lumps, I don't know how long she'd had them, but a while, and then she'd gone to the doctor who comes to the island every couple of weeks, and DD said he told her he couldn't know for sure, but they were probably cancer. He said they'd have to make an appointment for her to have a biopsy. Then he said she also might have AIDS, "because of her chosen lifestyle," he said. I asked her what he saw that pointed to AIDS, and she said, "How should I know? He was kind of a dick about it." So, that was ... odd.

I can tell you ... I can say that she was in a lot of pain. The lumps were putting pressure on her, and that was causing a chronic ache that sometimes intensified into something sharper, if she'd been in the van too long, or was ... under stress. You could see it in her face when the pain was bad. She got pale and looked a lot older and she would stop talking, too. When you tried to talk to her, she'd raise her head and say, "Sorry? What were you saying?" as if she'd been concentrating on an internal dialogue with the pain. She was smoking hash when she could get it, and she had some pain pills, too, but she didn't like taking those except to sleep, because she felt they affected her playing.

We were touring eastern Canada, DD, Pete, and I, and she was in rough shape. But she wanted to play so bad, to complete the tour. It was something she felt she had to do, tour one last time, play to those audiences with us, because she really didn't know if she'd ever get to do it again. Sometimes I'd look at her and just want to cry, especially when we were playing together, and we'd be connecting like we do, and she'd be playing so beautifully that I just wanted to soak up that beauty and keep it with me always, to keep the beauty of her playing at the front of my mind, not as a memory. She'd catch me looking at her like that and she'd just roll her eyes, as if to say, "Oh, fer crying out loud, it's still me, ya know. Don't drive me nuts looking at me like a drowned runt puppy." She didn't like me seeing her being weak. It's funny, I guess I do have a problem where I take Pete for granted. I always thought my connection with DD was stronger than his; that's probably arrogant but it's what I thought. But I guess I was probably mistaken in some ways because when she was really, truly sick, I mean when it was the end of the night and she'd pushed herself as far as she could go and she could barely walk, it was actually Pete that she turned to.

I remember going up to the hotel early after one of the shows. I was almost asleep when I realized that I had left my kobza out in the hallway — I had put it down to go through my many pockets to find the hotel key, but then when I did finally find the key, I forgot my instrument was there — and it had probably been lying out there for an hour or so. I went out and there was Pete way down the hall, physically carrying DD in his arms to her room. I saw them but I don't think they saw me, and I probably should have thanked him for doing that, but strangely I was afraid that he'd feel insulted.

The next day I was considerably hungover, so I didn't have the energy to say anything about it. It felt awkward. So just for the record let me say that of all the men I've known in the touring life, Pete is the most decent, Good-with-a-capital-*G* man that I ever encountered on the road, and probably the most underrated, song-sensitive drummer maybe in the world. He's not a big guy, and he wasn't a kid anymore by then either, but he carried her in his arms. That's

Pete, right there. If every guy was like Pete, the world would be a lot better. If every drummer was like Pete, when you went to a show you'd be able to hear the words better in songs and understand better what they were actually about. You'd be lifted and brought low and lifted again by a rhythm that understands the idea behind every word, a rhythm that comes from a truly generous spirit.

Then we were in Toronto. Rosalyn was there making a record, and she was actually in the thing with Cole at that time. It was only a few months since the two of them had left their long-time partners and gone off with each other after years of carrying on this crazy un-secret affair. Cole wasn't actually in Toronto. I forget where he was, but he was on one of his never-ending tours of the American South or something. His quest for world domination. The thing was, he really didn't want Rosalyn to come to our show. He didn't want Rosalyn to see DD at all. He had an inkling that they'd been more than road buddies, and he knew about DD's reputation as the gateway lesbian; plus, before Rosalyn had got together with Cole, it was known that she'd had one of those "don't ask, don't tell" kind of relationships with Alistair. And Cole knew what a lying dog he himself had been for so many years, so he knew from the inside out how a person could appear for all intents and purposes to be an honourable, straight-shooting person and actually turn out to be an inveterate liar in their love life — and hell, Rosalyn didn't even *seem* like a person who would walk the straight and narrow, if you know what I mean. For Cole it was a kind of curse, a very common curse: his lack of trustworthiness made it difficult to trust others. And I'm not judging him for that. Or, if I am judging him, then I judge myself for judging him, because I have no right. I've also been untrustworthy. I have deceived. I have fucked up. But I try to trust anyway, out of a sense of fatalism, and self-abnegation — I understand that if I'm betrayed, well, I had it coming, didn't I? But, okay. Let's face it, I'm also a jealous person.

Cole didn't want Rosalyn seeing DD. And Rosalyn very much wanted to see DD, and DD wanted to see Rosalyn, and I wanted

DD to see Rosalyn. Because DD's like a sister to me, and Rosalyn is at least a first cousin, maybe a sister, too. And we all thought, well, maybe DD was dying. It just didn't seem right to let jealousy get in the way of a dying sister being with her best friend.

It surprised me that Rosalyn was actually going to *obey* Cole and not come see DD. Rosalyn is not, as I think I mentioned, in the business of being told what to do. But Cole told her he wasn't comfortable with her seeing DD, and I think he maybe laid it down as an ultimatum — him or her. And the fact that Rosalyn was going to obey was a sure indication of the wrongness, in the end, of the two of them as a couple. Both of them had defined themselves, publicly, as people who did whatever the hell they wanted to do, whenever the hell they wanted to do it, so naturally there were going to be conflicts, compromises. But Rosalyn agreeing not to see DD out of subservience to Cole's wishes, that was just ... just wrong, wrong, wrong. Especially when DD was dying, for God's sake.

So, despite the fact that I had a big show, and I was extremely worried about whether I was prepared to play the new material — especially with my weak, clangy pronunciation of the Ukrainian verses (when I think of how my *rrr*'s sounded back then it gives me the shameful shudders), and I was sure the entire Ukrainian community of Toronto was going to judge me for it — I found myself dialing Cole's personal number and speaking to him for over an hour in an effort to persuade him to let my poor suffering sister see her friend.

I don't call Cole's personal number. It's just not something I do because I know he has a million people trying to get at him, to get him to do stuff for them. Managers who want him to take their bands on tour, groupie girls, people selling shit. So I don't use it. It was the first time I'd used it in years.

But he did listen to me. I guess it was because I don't bug him all the time, and because we had this history together going back a long way, having suffered through the same troubles with women connected to the road, and suffering through the public's general indifference to our music for the first couple of years, and then of course all the nonsense when Campbell Ouiniette "managed" both of us. And our great love for the song *Galveston* by Jimmy Webb.

People wonder why he and I are friends. He's a real man's man, and I'm … not. Yeah. He's a big, tough, rootin' tootin' real-life cowboy, as everyone knows.

Being a singer-songwriter, though, you can have a persona as a real man's man, but to be any good, you have to be good at things a lot of his fans might think of as, um, I don't know … womanly. Like connecting to your own feelings, needing to share them with other people, understanding and caring deeply about other people's feelings. Caring so much about another person's feelings that you want to try to put those feelings into words, to somehow see if you can understand them better. Even the losing feelings. Especially them. If you can't do that you're no good as a songwriter, and that's it. Sorry. Cole is good at these things that are supposed to be womanly, and I get that about him, without bugging him about it, and so maybe that's how it is that I'm friends with him. I could be wrong about that.

He was pretty embarrassed about his own feelings on the matter at hand. He knew it was ridiculously jealous to try to order your girlfriend not to see her sick friend. And he actually hadn't understood that she might be dying. Or he'd heard it and he hadn't believed it, but he seemed to believe me about it. He was also aware that his lack of trust came from his own untrustworthiness.

But it was funny; despite his own self-awareness, which is a quality I've always liked about him, he still wasn't relenting. He still just couldn't stand the idea of the two of them together, on a stomach-hurting level.

I told him this was understandable, given everything the two of them had gotten up to together, but in this case, I told him he was morally obliged to make an exception, on account of DD being in severe pain and *possibly dying.* He understood this, but he was still hanging on to his objection. I think partly because Rosalyn had waited quite a while before she copped to Cole about the, er, bedtime shenanigans that DD and Rosalyn had occasionally gotten up to.

For some reason I kept returning to the idea of faith, and to something I'd just heard in a movie, *The Verdict* with Paul Newman. (I like to watch movies from the seventies and eighties on the plane; the nostalgia helps calm my border-crossing and flying phobias.)

In the closing speech, Newman says, "In my religion, we are taught that if we don't have faith, we must *act as if we have faith. And faith will be given to us.*" My point with Cole being that in order for him to heal after the madness of his previous breakup and simultaneously take up with Rosalyn after the years of deception, he would have to *behave* as if he trusted Rosalyn, if he ever wished to *get* to a point where he could trust anybody. Fake it till you make it, so to speak. And to his every objection to trusting Rosalyn with DD, I would bring a variation on this notion. With a sprinkling of "but she may be *dying*, Cole."

After a while, I did ... grudgingly win him over. When Rosalyn did come down to the show for the last few songs, we hauled her up for an encore and we sang "Jackson" together. And then she and DD went off to some recording studio, and Rosalyn turned off her phone. And then Cole went nuts trying to reach her, eating his own innards with jealousy. I guess it would have been interesting for Jenn, that peerless woman he threw away for no good reason, to see him then. That was one piece of advice Cole didn't thank me for. I mean the part about letting Rosalyn see DD.

I suppose if she'd actually died, it wouldn't have been as bad. But when she got home, Miruna took her into the hospital in Vancouver to get a second opinion, and it turned out the lumps were growing but benign and could just be cut out. So, she wasn't dying. After all that.

What's peculiar is that she didn't actually disappear until after she found out she wasn't dying. That's odd, no? Or maybe it isn't. I don't always have a perfect grip on the distinction between what is weird and what is not weird, and I think my grip on that might be getting looser rather than tighter.

LILA AUSTIN

VIDEO SHOOT, SAN FRANCISCO, 2015

I DON'T KNOW. SHE JUST WENT. It was two days since she'd found out she wasn't dying, and she agreed to come out and play the Winnipeg Folk Fest with us, because it was a supposedly some ginormous important gig the label wanted everybody at. We were talking about what the setlist was gonna be like, and we were arguing, as usual, like always with those bitches. Nowadays I'm a solo act, I just sing the next song as it comes to me, and the band follows along. I mean they have to, because I'm in charge of this motherfucking ship, I'm the goddamn captain, and if I want to sing the goddamn "Good Ship Lollipop" by Shirley motherfuckin' Temple, that's what we're gonna *play*. But with the Johannahs it was always bitch, bitch, bitch, bitch. Kris had forgotten her silver Telecaster in Vancouver, and it wasn't there yet, so she didn't want to play the songs she liked to play on her Telecaster. And G was pushing her starfucker personal agenda, "Why don't we play *two* of my songs tonight instead of my token *one* song" — fuck me gently with a chainsaw. My position was, "Whatever. Nobody gives a fuck. They just wanna hear 'Hummingbird Café' again. Let's fucking give it to them and get the fuck out of Winnipeg."

I hate playing mainstage in Winnipeg, because I tell you — yeah,

yeah, sure, every musician in our little world wants to make it to mainstage Winnipeg Folk Festival on Saturday Night — but I'll tell you, you know who else wants to make it to the Winnipeg Folk Festival mainstage on Saturday Night? Fucking every goddamn mosquito in Manitoba. I swear to God. They see the light coming off that stage from *thousands* of miles away, and they come. It's a multi-generational *goal* for mosquitoes to get to mainstage Winnipeg Folk Fest on Saturday Night. It's something grampa and gramma mosquitoes tell their little mosquito grandchildren about when they tuck 'em into bed: "One day, little one, you are gonna get to that big light in the distance, and you are gonna fucking *feed* on the nice performers there. Those bags of blood are up there singing, making those positive vibrations, and you are just gonna eat them alive. It'll be so glamorous, you'll be feasting on that famous singer lady. Some of you, you go ahead and just fly into her *mouth* while she's singing a long, high, sustained note. You do that, little mosquito grandkids. One day. One day."

So, yeah. Great. Winnipeg Folk Fest. And we were all bitching each other out about the setlist, and DD said, "Hey, I'm just gonna grab some smokes," and she got out of the tour bus. She didn't take her suitcase but I should have known something 'cause she did have her fiddle case on her back.

What I believe? I think she stole a car. Cops never found any trace of her at the bus station, at the airport, the train station. There were no charges on her credit card. And I know she had an eye on this one car, this Oldsmobile. I don't know what kind it was, it was from the eighties or nineties. I just remember her sayin' something as we passed it, both times, on the way to the festival grounds. Like, "There's an Oldsmobile something-something. Most invisible car in the world. Total opposite of a heat score. My dad said you drive that model Oldsmobile, no cop ever gonna see you unless you're all over the road, crazy drunk. Most boring, unnoticeable car ever made." She said that. So, I think she stole an Oldsmobile and lit out onto the prairie side roads. I told the cops, "you look to see if a fuckin' Oldsmobile went missing," and they looked at me, like, "What kind of Oldsmobile?" and I said, "I don't fuckin' know, cop. A grey one," and the cop rolled his eyes at me. I was like, "Don't you roll your eyes at me, my friend is fucking missing!" That maybe was not the most diplomatic way to get them on the case, I guess. But I think that's what she did.

MIRUNA MOLNAR

FERRY FROM GALIANO ISLAND TO VICTORIA, 2016

MAYBE I HAD LOST HER ALREADY. I know she was with other women on the road. I know there was something with Rosalyn while we were together. Too many wacky postcards full of hearts arrived General Delivery, Galiano Island.

Maybe the routine of life, the letting the chickens out in the morning, the shopping for groceries at the same little store, the jaw-clenched little bickering arguments about how well a pot was washed or not that, sure, sometimes wound up with me punching a few holes in the wall, the diminishing frequency of sex … maybe that was all just a zombie love that was wandering around without knowing it was dead, and Melanie just put it out of its misery. But it felt at the time as if I began the day with a girlfriend, a love partner who called me *honey* and *my love*, and the neighbour came over for coffee after dinner and stole my life away. And I watched it happen like you do in a dream where someone is trying to smother you to death but you can't move. But after a nightmare like that you wake up and pump your lungs for a while and the nightmare is over. But this was a permanent, waking reality. And the way she did it was so.... I still don't really understand it.

We were out on the porch with the dog, having tea. DD was smoking her after-dinner hash chunklet in her little swirly glass pipe. I had cooked bacon, although I was a vegan before I met her. Like she always did after eating bacon, DD belched and sang, to the tune of "The Sounds of Silence," "Hello bacon, my old friend, it's pleasant tasting you again."

The dog barked. Then a voice from behind some shrubbery in our backyard said, "Hi, neighbour!"

And out of the bush jumped a girl. A woman. A woman in her late twenties. Tall, with blond hair that wasn't short and wasn't long. Athletically wiry. Not soft and curvy like me, like I thought DD liked her women. She was wearing denim overalls, a clean T-shirt, and workboots.

"Hi!" we said, together.

The dog ran up to her. "Hi, girl! How ya doing?" the woman said to her, letting her smell her hands then scratching her back vigorously.

"Who're you?" said DD, in her friendly, take-people-as-they-come way.

This new person leaped up onto the porch, offering DD her hand to shake.

"I'm Melanie. Dexie is my mom. I grew up here. I just got out of prison."

DD shook her hand super-friendly, without hesitation. "Howdy, neighbour!"

Melanie turned to look at me. She looked hungry to me, like a predator, right away. She offered me her hand. "Hi. I'm Melanie."

"I'm Miruna," I said. "This is DD."

"Oooh!" said Melanie, as if she was just realizing that we were two women who lived together, and all that entailed to her. As if it was saucy, somehow.

"Would you like some tea or coffee?" I asked, like a sucker. Like a fool who blunderingly helps to destroy all she has worked to build in her life.

"Coffee, coffee, coffee, coffee, coffee! Thank you! Can I sit down here on the porch?"

And that's what she did. Just sat down, easy as pie, cross-legged on the wooden porch. We were on our wicker couch and she was on the porch. And then she proceeded, in some way I still do not understand, to steal DD's heart, I guess. Beats me. I thought she was sketchy as hell. Twitchy. But there you go. No accounting for tastes. No accounting for the tastes of someone you've been with for three years and made a home with. No accounting for it.

DD asked her, "So, just got out of prison, eh?"

"Yup."

"What for?"

"Fraud!" So darn cheerful.

And of course DD always had to reflect the other person's attitude back at them.

"I love fraud!"

"Me, too," said Melanie. "Well, I used to. I'm going straight now. I'm here on my mom's vouching, so I can't get into no trouble or she'll lose the house."

"Good for you."

"Still, there really is no feeling in the world like leaving a high-end shopping mall loaded with expensive clothes you bought with somebody else's credit card."

"I bet."

"I mean, credit cards come with insurance and all. You're just ripping off the insurance companies, not a person or anything."

"Right."

I tried to be empathetic. "What led you to get into all that?"

"Well," she said, "the love of my life killed himself. I kind of went crazy for a few years. That's how I turned to crime."

"Wow. That's awful."

"Yeah. It was awful. I started off stealing stuff that was just lying around in bars when I was drunk. Then before I knew it, I was raiding the yachts around here and taking the goods in my truck to sell in Victoria."

"Whoa."

"Yeah. I just went crazy. I'm doing better now though."

"So, what are you gonna do now that you're back?"

"Well, I can't leave the island except in the company of my mom. I've got one of these ..." She rolled up her pant leg to show one of those electronic house-arrest ankle bracelets. "It calls the home phone every hour or something, and if I'm not around the parole officer calls. Also, they can come visit any time. Although I kind of doubt they'll come that often seeing as how I'm on an island."

I tried to stay empathetic. "I'm so sorry you lost the love of your life." I put my arm around DD.

"Yeah, it was crazy. He had always had depression. He had attempted before. But I never really thought he would do it. I just lost it. I went crazy. I wasn't in my right mind, for, like, years."

We knew her mom, Dexie. We bought goat cheese from her. She was an old hippy lady, an ex-American, who'd come here with her draft-dodger boyfriend in the seventies. She hadn't mentioned that she had a daughter in prison, but I guess that might be a hard thing to broach with new neighbours.

"I guess now I'm gonna work around the property. I'm just so glad to be out, you know? I feel like I have a ton of energy to burn. I'll probably build a couple new outbuildings. Maybe a small barn, a tool shed, a little one-room cabin for myself."

"Cool. We could help out on that if you need somebody to hammer a few nails."

I wanted to say, "Speak for yourself! I've got way too much on the go right now to build other people's tool sheds," but somehow I didn't. Something about her was really rubbing me the wrong way. Maybe her cheerful way of talking about ripping people off, and the cheerful way DD was just accepting her cheerfulness.

"I love how accepting you guys are. I can feel you're not judging me. A lot of people been judging me around here since I got out." She hugged herself.

Then DD asked her, "Ever do that thing where you take the tags off cheap things at Walmart and put them on super-expensive things?"

Melanie brightened. "Yeah, all the time! That was a good one. I fuckin' hate Walmart anyway."

"Me, too."

They were getting along like a house on fire. It was just great. I went to do some cleanup in the kitchen. I could hear them chatting and laughing as I scrubbed a pan that wasn't properly cleaned. DD told her one of her old anecdotes about how when she was a teenager she hacked into the Canadian Imperial Bank of Commerce website and made it dole out a fifty-dollar bill from the cash machine across the street from her high school every lunch hour. God I do not miss hearing that story.

They were just laughing about crime like old friends. I couldn't stand it and I went back out on the porch. Melanie was stroking our dog behind her ears.

"Anyway, I'm not the only jailbird on this island. You girls know about John Marshall?"

"Yeah," said DD.

"Not me." I looked at DD. "John who's down at the store all the time with the camo cap? He's been to prison?"

"Not for very long," said DD, as though, given how short a stint he'd done, it really wouldn't have been worth mentioning to me.

"What?"

"Yeah. That little campground he runs on his property, he had a pen inside the shower that was really a camera. He was videoing the girls. Pret-ty slea-zy."

I looked at DD. "Really?"

"Yep."

"Jesus."

"Yep."

"How long did he get?"

"Not long," she said. "About three months. He was sort of on parole for a while after that."

I was shocked. "But he still rents out that camping space to people every summer. Shouldn't there be an order against him not to rent it to girls or something?"

"Yeah, there should. But there ain't."

"Oh my God." I shivered at the thought of going into a shower and having some dirty old man watching me on his computer. "I kind of wish somebody had told me about him before now."

"Sorry, babe. I forgot."

"You forgot that John was a peeping Tom?"

"Naw. I forgot I hadn't told you already." She took a hit off her pipe then offered it to Melanie. She knew I didn't want any.

"Aww, thanks for the offer. I can't. They pee test me, randomly."

"That sucks."

"Totally. All I have to get endorphins with is exercise, video games —" Then she looked right at DD and said, "and playing with myself about five times a day."

The way she looked at DD when she said that, I just about slapped her across the face right there. "Well, it's great to have you over to visit. . . ." I said instead. God why *didn't* I hit her right then and there?

Anyway, who cares. It wouldn't have helped.

After Melanie left I suppose I said something disparaging about her and that seemed to really bug DD. She told me I was judging people when I didn't understand what they might be carrying. I said, "Well, whatever, I can think whatever I want about somebody," and she was like, "Well, I guess you can but you might know a couple of other people who've had trouble with the law and trouble with drugs and maybe taken a few things."

And I said, "Are you saying I'm judging you?" and she said, "No, of course not. Let's just drop it."

I said, "Do you want to talk about it?"

And she said no, we could talk about it later.

You wanna find Melanie? Good luck. She's long gone. Left the island the same summer DD disappeared. Left her little electronic anklet behind, left her mother on the hook to pay a ten-thousand-dollar bond. Draw whatever conclusions you want. I did. Look, I'm trying to move on from all this. That's all I have to say.

MELANIE SCHIFF

ALOUETTE CORRECTIONAL CENTRE FOR WOMEN, 2016

DD, DD, OF COURSE I REMEMBER DD. She's the reason I'm here. I mean, yeah, yeah, I'm responsible for my own actions. I'm the one who made the decision to break parole and then do all that other stuff. I'm the person responsible for my life. They make you say stuff like that here. Of course, of course, it's true. It's good stuff. Good stuff. Listen, do you have a cigarette? ... Oh, okay. Yeah, good for you.

It's not all super clear to me how it all went down. It's a blur, and when I started mixing in the vodka I got some wicked blackouts. Have you ever come out of a blackout and you're having sexual intercourse with somebody? That is the worst, I'm telling you. Good times.

But now I'm on the right track. I'm clean and sober and *loving it!* I get so much out of just life these days. I love music. I love helping out with the babies here. Did you know there's babies here? So cute! I just wanna squeeeze them up! Love the babies. [Singing] *I believe the babies are the future! Teach them all and let them lead today!*

Yeah, I guess they picked me up somewhere in the north of B.C. We had a parting of the ways. Okay, well, these days I'm totally taking responsibility for my actions, so, I admit, it was at least half or even the majority, like sixty percent, my fault that we had a parting of the ways.

See, I was not supposed to be using *drugs* when I was out on supervision, there. And I wasn't, most of the time, but *every now and then* I fell off the wagon before I got back on the wagon again. It came in through the garbage truck. Yeah, I had a job doing all the recycling stuff, loading the truck. Which was good, because it got me active, outdoors, which is what I'm suited to. It got me moving. But the bad part was I kind of *persuaded* the guy who drove the truck off the island to bring me back a little care package when he came back from dumping the stuff in the Big Smoke. I still had friends who were using back then, and they lived there in Victoria, and it was just too easy. It was too easy for me to fall into old patterns of behaviour.

It came in through the garbage truck, and that's how I left the island, with the rest of the garbage. Ha ha! No, I shouldn't talk shit about myself, because that's not constructive or productive. But that's how I left the island.

DD and I had been emailing. I guess some of it got [singing] *kinda dirty*. And then she told me that for various reasons she was gonna disappear for a while. She said some people were going to "adopt" her, and I don't know how that could have been since she was, you know, a grown-up, sort of, but she said she was going to disappear and try to find one last good place in the world to be. And I said that sounded good to me, and that I really needed to find some kind of good place. I told her I had been really close to using again and it scared me.

And that was probably the crux of the matter, that I left out the part that I was already using again. I kinda thought she would understand, how sometimes you say things that are not true, but that are the way you wish they could be, so that you can maybe get to where they are true. She said she'd had her own problems with coke and stuff, but when she picked me up at the terminal in Tsawwassen, I told her I just had to make a couple of calls and see a couple of people before we headed off the beaten path together like we were planning.

I probably should have known she would know what was going on, but, anyway, I popped in to these guys' apartment for a few minutes and I told her I was just saying goodbye. But she started to act all suspicious and everything, and getting all grumpy and saying, "Gee, you sure spent a long time in the bathroom back at that rest stop, what were you up to in there?" I was like, "I'm just having my period, geez," and she just stared ahead at the road in this big old car we were driving in. I asked her where she got it and she pretended not to hear me.

We got a room at some Super 8. I don't actually know where we were driving, isn't that funny? I think she was maybe already not trusting me with important information. And I was in the can for a long time, and when I came out she was sitting on the bed, looking at me.

And she said something like, "Listen, I need you to be straight with me here." I interrupted and told her I had really bad periods sometimes, and she said she just wanted to know if I really wanted to do this with her — if I really wanted to, I don't know, look at the Man in the Mirror and [singing] *make a change!* or whatever. I said I didn't know what she was asking me that for, of course. But obviously she was on some kind of trip where she was like, [singing] *Baby! I'm gonna be the one that saves you!* and I just found that kinda patronizing at the time.

We must have gone a long way, because it felt like we were driving forever. Like, days. And I wasn't sleeping. But finally we got to I-don't-know-where. Prince George? Fort Rupert? Fort Macleod? Wherever. And she caught me calling some guys and talking to them about sending me a care package, because I was really feeling shitty. Super shitty. Dark. I told her I really needed to sleep. She helped me out; we smoked a *ton* of hash and watched TV on the motel bed, and just cuddled. I remember her saying, "Just promise me you won't hitchhike around here. Get on a bus, steal a car, but don't hitchhike." I was like, sure, whatever baby, although I guess I was so stoned it didn't click that if I was gonna be thinking about hitchhiking, she was probably planning on leaving me flat. I don't remember her saying goodbye. I guess I passed out, and then it was afternoon and she was gone.

She left me *some* money, but I still felt like she totally abandoned me, after luring me out of my parole situation. I just cried and cried over what a mess I'd made out of my life, and then I went out there to the bar in that little dump of a town and just partied down till I woke up in a holding cell. Eventually they figured out the deal, and I went to remand, then I went to court, and then I wound up here. I have just over six months to go and then we'll see if my mom is up for taking me back again. I feel bad about her losing the property because of me, but of course it was as much mine as hers to lose. Besides, she's got a pretty nice place she's renting, and she kind of owes me, in ways I don't feel like saying. Just put it this way: I have not had an easy life. Some people like DD lead charmed lives, get all the luck. I'm still waiting for my luck to come my way, but that's wrong. I'm responsible for my own life, and I'm serious about taking responsibility for my choices.

EPILOGUE

BY GEOFF BERNER

AFTER I HAD ASSEMBLED AND EDITED down the reams of material I had collected about DD, I was still no closer to finding her than before. But at least I had a thing to show to people. I started passing around the manuscript to some writer friends. Within a few days, several of them had called me to point out all the clues that made it likely that DD had gone to Haida Gwaii. Apparently it was obvious.

Following that tip, I booked myself a flight to Queen Charlotte City on Haida Gwaii, formerly (*temporarily*, *erroneously*, the Haida would say) known as the Queen Charlotte Islands.

I stayed at a guest house in Masset. I didn't really know where to start looking for DD. I'm not a police detective.

I started drinking at a certain bar in Masset every night. I bought people beers, but I tried not to be ostentatious about it. Not "a round for the bar!" kind of drink-buying. I brought my Italian accordion, Estella, in her old Dutch leather and wood case. When I felt ready, I took Estella out of the case and started playing. At first I just played the instrument, and then I sang a few of my odd little songs.

It happens that once people have heard my odd little songs, sometimes they start to trust me with their stories. They understand from my songs that I know there are things in the world that most people would rather not talk about but that are important. This approach to getting to know strangers has worked with me in Romania, Belfast, rural Alberta, New York, etcetera. I use carefully written words and music to expose my true feelings to strangers in a manner that seems careless, and in this way I connect with them.

I met a couple. A man and a woman in their thirties. She was partly Japanese Canadian, and he was Haida. They lived in a house together down a long old logging road. They had two children who had sleepovers at their grandmother's house every Tuesday, and they caught much of their food by walking down to the beach in the morning. After I shared a song that is partly about my mother, partly about a girl I loved when I was young, partly about the disappeared women on the Downtown Eastside of Vancouver, and partly about the Shoah, all at the same time, the couple decided to drink with me a while.

After the third shot of whisky, and a very old song about missing your hometown but knowing that you can never go back there, they asked me what I was doing on Haida Gwaii. I told them that I was looking for a woman, a violinist I played music with.

The thing is, if you play your song that is partly about your mother, partly about a girl you loved when you were young, partly about the disappeared women on the Downtown Eastside, and partly about the Shoah, all at the same time, people don't ask you if you're a cop or something when you start asking around about the whereabouts of people.

She asked, "What steps are you taking to find her?"

I said, "You're looking at the steps."

They both nodded.

They said that they both made a point of only going to the bar on Tuesday nights, but they could make some quiet inquiries. If I was there the following Tuesday, they might or might not have some information for me. I said that was perfect for me, and I would be there.

I spent the next week walking around in the woods, trying to drink less, trying to do some writing on the book about DD and mostly not writing anything. I was chatting with the husband of the lady who runs the guest house. They are in their early sixties. I had heard a rumour in the bar that he had spent some time in prison. He made tea for me.

"So, what are you going to say to your friend if you find her?"

"I don't know."

"What are you going to do if you don't find her?"

"I don't know that either. Probably nothing, I guess."

"Why is it important that you find her?"

Then it occurred to me that he might know DD. I don't why. I normally don't make eye contact with people when I'm talking with them, because looking at them distracts me from my thoughts about what they're saying and this distraction also prevents me from being able to think of what I want to say to them. A lot of people are put off by this. When he asked, "Why is it important that you find her?" it made me look up from my hand, which I had been fiddling at with my other hand. I looked at his face.

I studied his face to see if there was a clue there. Was I just imagining something in his tone of voice that suggested he knew where she was, that he actually knew her quite well, some kind of mark of DD on him? I couldn't tell. I only suspected, without evidence.

"Why is it important that I find her?"

"Yeah."

"Do you mind if I take a little time to think about the answer before I answer that?"

"Take as much time as you need." There was an ironic look on his face when he said the word *time* that made me think that he might be thinking about the special nature of time in a prison.

I thought about his question for a while. We were both silent as I thought about it. Then I said something like this:

"Well, I don't know for sure that it's important that I find her. And I don't know for sure, if it *is* important, exactly *why* it's important.

When I start a project, like a song or a book or a tour of a country, I start with a feeling that I somehow ought to do something, but I don't always know why. Sometimes I play a song that I've just written, and the audience reacts a certain way, and I react a certain way to it myself, while I'm playing it, and I realize only then why I had to write the song. But sometimes I play a song hundreds of times, and only when I get to a certain bar in a certain town and someone is in the audience who really needs to hear it, *that's* when I know why I did the thing. Or sometimes it just hits me out of nowhere. This looking for DD is kind of like that. Also, I certainly don't know for sure that it's good and right for me to find DD right at this moment. That's not for me to say. I do feel it would do no harm for DD to *know* that I'm looking for her, and after letting her know that, I'd be satisfied to let her make up her mind about what to do about it. Do you know what I mean?"

He nodded. He told me that he understood what I was saying and asked if I wanted more tea. I said thanks but no because I already needed to take a piss.

The next Tuesday I went to the bar and ordered a beer. Some people who had been there the week before asked if I had brought my accordion but I hadn't. I didn't feel like it that day.

Eventually, the couple from the previous week showed up. They said there was a guy who might or might not know DD and he wanted to meet me. They told me to come to their house the next day. We had a couple more beers, and they talked about all the things that had washed up on the beach from Japan after the tsunami. A lot of garbage, Styrofoam, and even a motorcycle. Of course nobody wanted the motorcycle because everyone figured it was probably radioactive. People worried about the food from the sea, too, but they couldn't really do anything about it because that's what people ate there. I had a shot of whisky for the road and then I walked home to the guest house.

The next day I drove to the couple's house. Their kids were at school. They gave me coffee and told me that the guy's name was Jim.

He was waiting out on the beach to take a walk with me.

Jim was probably in his sixties. He was a Haida guy, wearing shorts and sandals and a T-shirt. He shook my hand.

"I came to tell you something."

"Okay."

"I'm telling you that DD is somewhere. She's with us."

"Okay."

"She has a lot of healing to do. Some people really messed her up. And no one stepped up to protect her. It was wrong."

"I agree with what you're saying."

"Oh, you do?" He sounded wary and somewhat offended.

"Yes."

"I don't care if you agree with me or you don't agree with me."

I really tried hard to think of the right thing to say to that. "I understand."

"Oh, you do?"

"I think I understand."

"You think so?"

"If I'm wrong, it won't be the first time."

"No, probably not."

"Definitely not."

"Okay then." He paused for a few moments then spoke: "I have a message from DD for you."

"Okay."

"She says don't worry about her for now. She's doing what she's supposed to be doing. You can stop looking for her and go back to doing your work that you know you're supposed to be doing. She says get back to work, Berner."

"Oh. Okay."

"She says she knows she's going to play music with you again, but she doesn't know exactly when. But in the meantime, don't worry about finding her. She'll let you know when the time comes. 'Get back to work, Berner.' She said for me to tell you."

"Okay. Thank you."

"Do you want me to try to get a message to her?"

"Sure. You can tell her that I understand."

"Oh, you do?"

I fixed him with a look in his eyes, which I almost never do. "Yes. I'm certain that I do."

"All right, then. I'm gonna go. Nice to meet ya."

He shook my hand and walked down the beach. I turned back in the direction I'd come.

ACKNOWLEDGEMENTS

This book certainly could not have been written without the help of the following people: Wayne Adams, Ralph Allen, Michael Barclay, Margot Berner, Nancy Berner, Sarge Berner, Toby Berner, Shaughnessy Bishop-Stall, Dennis E. Bolen, Benny Bratten, Genevieve Buechner, Kerry Clarke, Kris Demeanor, Frazey Ford, Soressa Gardner, Tanya Gillis, Heather John, Donnacha Kirk, Corb Lund, Carolyn Mark, Justin Newall, C. Noyes, Stuart Parker, Sarah Rhude, Jess Shulman, Rae Spoon, Shannon Whibbs, Britt Zeidler, Karina Zeidler, Paulette Zeidler, Joseph Zeidler-Berner, and Ursula Nancy Zeidler-Berner.

Thank you for being indispensable.

As a special bonus, this novel comes with
Canadiana Grotesquica, a new original Geoff Berner album,
in downloadable high-quality digital format.
To access this album, go to www.geoffberner.com/grotesquica
and type in the following password:

UNJPMZGS